TIMBERJACK

In the rugged, towering Canadian forests, huge-muscled men settled their grudges with ax handles and bare fists.

Big Tim Chipman learned that the day he came back to claim his family's timber tracts. Ranged against him was Croft Brunner, whose hatred of the Chipmans had burned for twenty years.

So it was Chipman vs. Brunner, two big men battling for a lumber empire—and for Lynne Tilton, who was beautiful enough to be its queen.

TIMBERJACK

Dan Cushman

This hardback edition 1999
by Chivers Press
by arrangement with
Golden West Literary Agency

ISBN 0 7540 8053 6

British Library Cataloguing in Publication Data available

Printed and bound in Great Britain by
Redwood Books, Trowbridge, Wiltshire

TIMBERJACK

Chapter One

IT WAS no more than forty miles from the railhead at
Prince Albert to Vermilion Landing at the northern end
of Chilkoos Lake, but the paddle-wheel steamboat puffed
and splashed through most of the autumn day in making
it. At last the captain expended a quantity of precious
steam on one long toot of the whistle and came down
the steps from the hurricane deck, buttoning his blue
officer's coat.

"Vermilion Landing," he said to the boat's one passenger.

The passenger was in his middle twenties, a tall young
man with good shoulders and a face that would have
been handsome had it not been for a battered and
mended nose. He wore a red and gray plaid mackinaw,
stagged wool trousers, and logger boots, but the clothes

were all new, and there were less obvious things that set
him apart from the ordinary run of timber stiffs whom
he found making the journey. His hands, for example,
were big enough, but they lacked the timber worker's
broken, knuckly look, and he did not smell of hangover
from Prince Albert's saloons, either. It was the skipper's
experience that timber stiffs always smelled differently
going to Prince Albert than coming back. So there was
a deference in his manner not shown to ordinary stiffs
when he said:

"You heading back into the woods, you say?" He
waited for the young man to nod. "Well, I doubt
there'll be a train up the narrow gauge before tomorrow
morning, but see Ryan and he'll put you in the company bunkhouse. You'll have to get some blankets,
though."

"I'll get by."

He had a smile that the captain liked, so after thinking about it he said, "If you like, you can sleep here on
the boat. I won't be starting back before sunup."

"I'm in sort of a hurry."

"Heading for Talka, you say?"

He hadn't said. "Chipman."

The captain stood a trifle taller at hearing that. "Oh,"
he said, "Chipman!"

"The train still takes a man there, doesn't it?"

He meant it as a joke, and he was surprised when the
captain said, "I don't know."

The young man turned from the rail, where he had
been watching the docks, sheds, and houses of Vermilion
take shape from the blue-purple autumn mists of the
north country, and gave the captain a quick piercing
scrutiny. "Well, why in hell shouldn't it?"

"You'll have to see Burgess about that. He's over at
the company store." He pointed at one of the buildings, or the roof of one, for nothing except the lumber
storage sheds could be seen in its entirety from the lake.
"That's it, the one with the wind deflector on the stovepipe. You can see—"

"I know where it is."

"Oh, you've been here before?"

He nodded.

"I knew your face was familiar. When you got on the
boat, I said to myself, 'I've seen him before.' Over at

Mistook, that's where, I thought. I used to have the mail contract there."

He shook his head. "Chipman. Tim Chipman. I was raised in this country. Why, I rode this boat when I was a year old. Scotty Campbell was the skipper when I left."

"Oh, Chipman!" cried the captain, pretending to be very happy about it. Actually, his eyes showed that he was apprehensive. "I'm Jake Long. Of course I remember you. Who doesn't remember the Chipmans? I remember your dad real well. I remember him when I first came to the country. Well, so you're a Chipman!"

Chipman nodded and went on studying the town and the timbered shoreline. It pleased him to be somebody. The Chipmans might have slipped a little, but in that section of British Columbia the name still made people look at you. Here his father had built the first mill and sawed the first log, he had built the first big shed there in Vermilion, and Tim wasn't certain, but he believed he had been the first owner of this very boat they were afloat on.

"So you're a Chipman!" the captain repeated.

Tim Chipman kept looking at the town, its forested hills, and the hint of lofty mountains far away.

"Plan on a little visit, Mr. Chipman?"

"I'll be around a while."

"What business are you in?"

"Timber."

"Well, that's a Chipman for you. *Chip* off the old block!" he punned. "Didn't I hear you were a hockey player?"

"I batted it around a little."

"I guess so! The Maple Leafs!"

"No, I never played for the Leafs."

"Timber, eh?" He waited for him to volunteer more information. "Where are you operating?"

"Right here."

"Oh." He seemed to understand that he had said the wrong thing. "Of course, I know Chipman is still in business here. Well, I should say so. I guess we'll never see the day when the *Chipmans* don't get their logs out. Well, have to get ready to tie up. Good luck, Chipman."

The young man nodded. He was thinking that this fellow was probably employed by Croft Brunner, like everybody else. He had not failed to notice the captain's willingness to grovel for information, and whatever he learned, of course, he would trot to Brunner with.

His uncle Clay, he supposed, was having trouble with Brunner, but there was nothing unusual about that.

He lit a cigarette, spun the match away, and watched it bob in the lake for a couple of seconds before the boat, slipping easily with its power off, swung in toward the dock.

The Talka Company buildings were freshly painted a bright red with white trim. "TALKA RIVER TIMBER CO." read a sign mounted on the gable of the largest shed, facing the lake. He could remember Talka when it was a two-saw, one-whistle outfit operating over on the West Arm at Sista Landing, but that was long before Brunner took it over. You had to hand it to Brunner. You might hate his overbearing guts, but you had to admire him in a manner, too. He had more than a hard fist and a set of hobnails. He was smart—dollar smart.

The boat came to a stop with a shivering bump-bump of its side against the dock pilings. After some shouting back and forth between the boat and the dock, it was tied fast, and the old steam engine relaxed with a long hiss of relief, like a tired man letting his breath out. Then Tim could hear the silence of the great forest country disturbed only slightly by voices and the rumble of a hand truck that was being pushed from the warehouse. The smells of the country were there, too—pine needles, and freshly sawed lumber, and wood smoke.

He stirred himself then, put his plunder bag on his shoulder, lifted his suitcase, and walked down the landing stage.

"Good-by, Chipman," the captain called. "You say you're staying on?"

Tim Chipman felt like saying, Yes, you snooping bastard, I'm staying on. I'm here with nine hundred thousand dollars of Vancouver capital to rebuild Chipman Lumber and push that lousy Talka River outfit into the lake. Unfortunately, it was too far from being true. He was returning with $622 and some odd cents, all he had to show of the money his father had left him after three years in engineering school and four more playing wing for the Black Hawks.

"Yes, I'm staying on." The captain was still watching,

so he said, "If you see Brunner, give him my regards." Then, giving in to the impulse, "Tell him I have half a million in Vancouver capital to fix up the old mill. If he wants to sell out, tell him to come around and we'll talk business."

A damn-fool thing to say, but the slack-faced look of the captain left him feeling good all over.

The truth was, Tim Chipman did not know himself how long he would be there, or exactly why he had come at all. He had been in Minneapolis, just preparing to to take over the job of manager of an independent hockey club in North Battleford, when he received a telegram from Steve Riika, Clay's timber boss:

> YOU COME BACK NOW AND HELP TIM YOU
> COME BACK QUICK AND HELP CLAY.
> STEVE RIIKA

That was it. It sounded so much like big Steve that he could almost hear his Finlander accent. Tim laughed when he first received it and almost left for North Battleford anyway, but after he read it over he stopped laughing.

Something was bad or Steve wouldn't have sent it. So here he was home again, 622 bucks in his wallet, $2,000 worth of bridgework in his mouth, a dozen $18 shirts from Von Lengerke & Antoine, and a shaky knowledge of civil engineering to show for his journey "outside," as the men of the north woods still liked to call it.

Tall and broad-shouldered, he walked along the dock. New planking had been laid here and there. Some electric-light posts were new since his departure. A barge was loaded to its waterline with new-cut cedar bolts, waiting for the tug that would take it down the lake to Prince Albert and the spur line of the Canadian Pacific. He noticed that the butt end of each bolt carried the T and Circle brand of the Talka River Company. A second Talka barge stood empty—new but empty. Farther along were a couple of Chipman barges, planking warped and riding low from bilge. No Chipman logs or bolts. The Chipman loading equipment looked rusty and out of use. He left the docks and climbed the ramp to the corduroy that served as the town's main street.

The town wasn't much any more. When he was a boy this street had been a double line of keg and tin-cup saloons where almost any time of the day or night you could hear electric pianos banging and Swede and Finlander timberjacks having a good time. Now only one of the places was open, and it didn't have a customer. The old two-story hotel was boarded up. A store, the Vermilion Mercantile and Trading Company, was still open for business. It was freshly painted in the Talka red and white, so he would have known, even without the captain's word, that it was now Talka property. The sawmills, roofs visible to the west near the mouth of Vermilion River, were all quiet. No smoke had risen from that direction for years. It had proved cheaper to raft the whole logs or send simple squared bolts to Prince Albert, and discontinue the costly lake steamers that once had plied the sixty miles of Chilkoos Lake, making it busy and colorful, giving towns like Vermilion a steamboat crowd and a timber crowd, each with its own hangouts.

Some Beaver Indians were seated in front of the store munching candy bars. They at least had not changed. They had not washed, either. He recognized one of the men to be old George Roastingstick, who once had worked as bargeman for his father, so he put his things down outside the door to shake hands after first saying, "How!" in the Indian manner. Then he went inside.

The interior was long and dim, filled with the moldy burlap, spice, and smoked-fish smells of trading posts in the north woods everywhere. He stopped to get the flicker of late-afternoon brightness from his eyes. Someone was walking with a heavy tread he could feel across the floor. The man emerged between two cases and looked at him. Bill Burgess. Burgess had grayed slightly at the temples, but he was still broad and powerful, and judging by the way he moved, his feet were flat as ever.

"Hello, Bill," Tim said.

Burgess blinked rapidly several times and said, "Well, I'll be damned! I didn't recognize you. You're Tim Chipman."

"Have I changed that much?" Tim gave him a good smile. He still looked like a kid when he smiled. "You haven't changed a freckle."

"Oh, I'm a little bit older." He shook out the muscles

of his shoulders to indicate that he was in fine shape for forty-four. He was trying to act jovial, but he was excited, and Tim could see the rapid beat of the artery at his temple. "I was thinking of you just the other day. Yes, I was." He became very serious now. "I got to wondering whether anybody sent for you."

Jolted by his manner, Tim asked, "What happened to Clay?"

"Why I naturally thought you knew."

"No."

"Well." He just said that and thought about it before going on. After all, he owed his job to Croft Brunner, like the boat captain did. Neither of them wanted to be caught saying the wrong thing to a Chipman.

Tim said, "I got a crazy wire from Steve Riika. I don't know a thing about what happened."

"He didn't tell you about Clay?"

"No, damn it, no!"

Bill stalled for a while, getting his black sleeve protectors into a position that suited him. "He got hurt, you know."

"How badly?"

"I don't know. I haven't heard lately."

"What happened?"

"I guess there was a fight of some kind, but nobody that came through here seemed to know. They found him out there alongside one of those old skid roads by the river. That's what somebody told me. I guess he'd been beaten around the head and shoulders. They didn't come down here for help, or send to P. A. They brought a doc over from Chinook Inlet. Anyhow, that's what I heard. I wouldn't know, I didn't see him."

"Chinook!"

"Flew him across. I heard they landed a pontoon ship in one of the pond backwaters by the old mill, but when they tried to haul him out, the plane wouldn't take off, so they decided to leave him there. Mind you, this is all hearsay. One of the Injuns was telling me this. But you know how an Injun is—never gets anything straight."

Burgess was lying. That, or there was something he wasn't telling. He was sweating, and it wasn't warm enough for that. He was talking too fast and gesturing too hard.

"What happened to him?" A rough note had crept into Tim's voice.

"I told you—"

"I heard what you told me! I'm waiting for what you haven't told me. Now what the hell happened to him?"

"Now, Tim—"

"Who slugged him?"

"Listen here, Chipman, don't you come around to this place yelling at me. I don't have to take it. Maybe there was a time when people in this part of the timber had to take that kind of dirt from you Chipmans, but that time is gone."

"You're working for Brunner!"

"It's nobody's affair who I'm working for. If it happens to be Brunner, all right. It's nobody's business who owns this store. A Brunner dollar is as good as anybody else's dollar. It's legal and honest and the taxes are paid. I know you Chipmans had your trouble with him, and maybe you're having it yet, but that's no skin off my body. If you want to know what happened to Clay—"

Burgess had been edging around the counter and now he was behind it. His hands were out of sight. There he felt safe and he took a deep breath, but Tim reached across with a pouncing quickness that surprised him. He seized him by the front of his shirt; he dragged him, lifted him halfway over the counter.

Burgess had a slung shot in his hand, and in that poor position he tried to bring it around and slug his way free. Chipman was ready for it. He deflected the blow with an upraised left forearm. He seized the slung shot and tore it away. It was a thick strap of moosehide with several ounces of lead shot sewn in a pocket at one end.

Burgess was helpless for a few seconds with his feet off the floor and the side of his body across the counter. Then he got twisted around so his hands and one knee were braced and tried to make a fight of it. Although built solidly, he was fifteen pounds lighter than Tim, and that was too much. Tim dragged him forward and dumped him to the floor, which he hit with a solid thump that knocked the resistance out of him, and there he lay on his back, braced on his elbows, looking up into Tim's face.

"Did Brunner get to him?"

"What?"

"I asked if Brunner got to him."

"I don't know what happened."

"What are you trying to cover up?"

"Nothing!"

"Bill—"

"I know nothing but what I told you. If you and Brunner have stirred up the old feud, that's none of my affair. I just shovel beans in this dump and mind my own business. Brunner don't ask me for *my* advice."

Tim Chipman knew it was the truth. He stepped back. He was still holding the slung shot. He tossed it back across the counter. The bit of violence had burned off the edge he had felt since talking with the captain. He felt slightly ashamed of himself.

"Yeah," he said, "what in hell am I slapping you around for? You just take his orders."

He went back outside. The Indians were staring at him with their dark silence. He put his plunder bag on his shoulder and took up his suitcase. Then he stood wondering what his next move should be.

There was no train at the railroad shed, but he could get to the back country with a handcar, and the exercise would do him good.

Starting away, he glanced back through the smoky windows of the store and saw Bill Burgess cranking furiously at a wall phone.

Chapter Two

THE RAIL LINE ended among a maze of sidings at a turntable shed among the old mills. It was almost a mile. As he walked with his long, woodsman's stride he thought about his uncle Clay, and about Brunner.

Brunner had been log boss for Tim's father when they were timbering off that big stand of white on the Rouge River. Twenty-two—that was his age at the time. It wasn't often you found a boss logger aged twenty-two, but Croft Brunner was no ordinary man. He looked older, but that was his age. Tim's father, Pat, used to brag about it. He had been proud of Brunner, almost as if he were his own son. "There's a man that'll go places," Pat used to say, and in that he was correct. Brunner was the kind of man who would drive his crew until they were too tired to eat, doing more work than any of them. Then he used part of his sleeping time to work on his endless correspondence courses. In accounting, business correspondence, structural drafting, French, and pulp- and papermaking. Brunner had made his way in the world from the time he was twelve. He had never graduated from grammar school, but in many ways he was highly educated. One of the courses he never took, however, was Common Honesty and Ethics. Perhaps the International Correspondence School had no such course. At any rate, soon after five million board feet of Chipman saw logs disappeared in a rafting operation across Chilkoos Lake, old Pat learned by way of a friend in Vancouver that Brunner had invested in a wildcat saw called Saskatoon Mills, Limited, located over on the West Arm, and so he went out looking for him. They met at a campfire on the mouth of the Rouge, where Brunner and half a dozen of his rafting crew were drying off after being dunked in the lake.

Pat called him a thief that night, and Brunner responded by smashing the teeth loose all along one side of Pat's upper jaw. With Pat lying half in the fire, Brunner went on to give him the hobs in the time-honored lumberjack style. He had an uncontrollable temper and he might have killed Pat if the others had not pulled him off. As it was, Pat was never the same again. He coughed blood and that winter he contracted pneumonia. He recovered from that, but his health was broken, and he was found dead at the foot of a rollway a year later. There was talk of foul play, and an inquest, but it was probable that the old man had simply collapsed and rolled to the bottom; his bruises and broken bones would have been a natural consequence. After all, why would anyone have killed the old man? There was no fight left in him.

Brunner, of course, had gone his own way after that night on the Rouge. He worked openly with Saskatoon for a time, reorganizing it, bankrupting it. There was considerable speculation as to where the money went, and when Brunner commenced quietly buying up timber tracks, the speculation was put to rest. He was for a time representative for a Winnipeg pulpwood outfit, and later he bought interests in the Swiftwater Company and Talka Mills, both of which were having bad days because of the low lumber prices of the depression. Brunner now gave both a boost by leasing to them some cut-over lands he had bought at a song, and buying the second-growth stuff for his pulp concern. Chipman, unfortunately, had nothing like that to keep it going, but Clay kept operating year after year, always on a smaller scale, accounting it good times when he just broke even. Now that lumber prices were good again, and had been ever since the war, Chipman should have been turning a good profit, but Tim knew it wasn't. Clay still operated as though the year were 1920.

The railroad was a narrow-gauge affair that had been built by the Chipman, Talka, and Swiftwater companies forty years before. The depot was locked. He could find no one at the repair sheds; neither of the line's two locomotives was there.

He rolled a handcar from the tool house, and when still no one showed up, he started pumping from town. He turned for one last look before entering the spruce timber that hid the town from view, and saw Burgess and the Indians standing at the side of the store platform, watching him. He lifted an arm in farewell, but Burgess made no response. A few seconds later he was surrounded by the shadows and sweet odors of the forest.

The sun still touched him here and there as the rail line unwound in gentle curves, but there was no heat in it. The air had a feel of frost. A breeze sprang up, moving down from the north, carrying the chill of snow fields. Winter was not far distant. And soon he began to notice some edgings of snow along the timber of the higher hillsides.

The grade steepened. He had been moving rather easily, operating the handcar with first one arm and then the other, but now he had to bend to the task. He did not mind. It was good to test his muscles and empty the air sacs of his lungs.

The road here skirted a steep-sided gulch. The line, he noticed, was in good shape, the rails newly spiked, with fresh ties and stretches of new grade here and there. The shine of the rails indicated they had been carrying a good tonnage. After another five miles he passed through a short tunnel and came out on Vermilion River, a blue-gray stream with frequent stretches of white water, and here, blue in the wide valley, lay the smoke of Talka mill.

He grew tense and watchful, remembering the phone call Burgess had made. There was just a chance that one of Brunner's men might try to stop him. He came to a switch. It was open. He got off to lift the handcar to the main line. If he hadn't been familiar with the railroad, he wouldn't have recognized it as the main line; it was covered with rust. He pumped on through a V in the flank of a hill and came out with Talka camp before him.

It had grown. There were two mills now, although only one seemed to be in operation. One locomotive stood cold in a shed; the other was chuffing along with three empty flatcars while a man ran ahead to throw a switch. A big tractor and trailer outfit was grinding slowly down a rust-colored dirt road from the hills, laden with logs. Some stacks of timber stood beneath a drying shed, but for the most part the mill had been turning out squared bolts that would go elsewhere for sawing and finishing. A dam held back the river, forming a millpond of considerable size, but only some small drift stuff had been caught on the wire rope and pontoons of the boom. The old two-story office building was unchanged except for the coat of red and white that had become the Talka Company colors. Farther on, between the office and the silent mill, was the town—some fair-sized houses, some cabins and shacks, a wangan house, and the bunkhouses.

Men were about but none within a hundred yards, and no one paid the slightest heed as he pumped by on the handcar.

He passed the one-room depot with the name "Talka" on it, the signal tower with both its arms out. Beyond, the track settled into a cut through glacial gravels. The grade increased still more. He pumped with steady strokes. Fatigue settled in his muscles. Fatigue and deep breathing in the cool air did something to his senses, glazing them, and he pumped in a trance. Then he snapped out of it abruptly with the realization that there was an obstruction in the tracks.

A cribwork of logs had been laid across the line. Three men were there. One of them shouted to him to halt. He was a short, stocky man with a half-inch tangle of black whiskers and a big chew of tobacco in one side of his mouth. A second man, a huge, flat-faced blond, came toward him at a plodding shuffle like a grizzly bear walking upright. The third one was a skinny, pimply-faced kid of eighteen or nineteen who remained seated on top of the pile of cribbing with his nose in a comic book.

"Har, noo!" said the big fellow, with a Swedish accent. "You stop har, noo!"

"What the hell?" said Tim Chipman, although he knew well enough that the call from Burgess had brought them out to stop him. He let the handcar stop and kicked the foot cleat in to keep it from rolling back with the grade.

"Where you tank you're going?" the big Swede asked. He stopped and set himself as if to meet the unexpected charge of the handcar. He had an ax handle in one hand. He got one fist doubled and the ax handle ready, both in front of him. His face was set and obstinate. His nose had been beaten flat with his cheeks, and his eyes were only slightly depressed. All this made his face look vast and almost featureless. He had not tanned, but had turned pink with the weather. He had a chew of snoose in his lower lip, making it stick out like a scoop shovel and revealed his small, snoose-browned teeth. His ears were small and one of them had been chopped in half by hobnails. His age might have been twenty-five or it might have been forty; as with many huge men, it was impossible to guess.

After letting Tim look him over, he said, "Hey, what the hell, noo, don't you understand English language, hah?"

Tim said, "Get that timber off the track."

"Where you going with that handcar? That bane Talka handcar. Yah, that Talka brand, by golly. By yimminy, I call police, you take Talka handcar."

Tim walked around him and up the track. He took a look at the cribwork. The black-whiskered one stood with a half grin, watching him. The pimply-faced kid kept reading his comic book. It was a ragged book, and it had a picture of a space ship blasting off on the river. The logs had been set to break the ram of a locomotive without derailing it, and judging by the weeds grown up among them, they had been there for most of the summer.

"Why don't you just back off and ram through it?" asked the black-whiskered one.

"Whose idea was this?"

The man shrugged and made a noncommittal gesture down the track.

"Brunner?"

"Ask the boss," he said, jerking his head at the Swede. "He speaks better English than I do. Hey, Ole!"

"What you talking about?" asked the Swede. He got between them. He looked dumb and truculent. "I'm the boss har."

The black-whiskered man spat tobacco, wiped his lips on the back of his hand, and said, "Sure, you're the conductor. Ask to see his ticket."

Ole thought it over. It took a certain time for a thought to set itself in his brain. He decided this was funny. "Ho, ho! Yah. You got ticket, hah?"

Chipman said, "Get that stuff out of the way. This line is a third owned by Chipman and I know my rights. You keep it blocked and I'll have you down in Vancouver with a lawsuit slapped on you for the last nickel and stick of timber that you own."

"No," said Ole. "This line don't go to Chipman any more. Ain't letting nobody through to Chipman any more. Go away, noo. Go on, go on, get hell away!"

Chipman called him a dumb Swede bastard.

Ole reared himself straight with the ax handle. "You know who you talking to? Hah? I bane Ax-Handle Ole. What do you think of that?"

"Never heard of you."

Ole almost swallowed his snoose. He blew out his breath. It smelled of cheap whisky. "You never har of Ax-Handle Ole? Where you coom from you never har tell of me? Listen, I bane strongest man in whole damn woods. You don't har everyone tell how I lift whole damn rear axle on truck and hold it for five minutes so driver change tire without using his yak?"

"Don't let him get away with that stuff. Of course he's heard of you," said the black-whiskered one, egging him on. The pimply-faced kid had lowered his comic book and was grinning at the fun.

"By golly, yah!" said Ole, standing like a gorilla. "I got damn good notion to tie knots in your neck."

"Sing him your song," both his companions started urging.

Whereupon Ole sang in a peculiar falsetto:

"My name it bane Yonson,
  I coom from Wisconsin,
I work in the hardwood stand,
  I ride to Shee-baggin
On Yim Hill's red wagon
  Wit' ax handle in my hand."

Then he filled himself hugely with air and, stamping his heavy hobnailed boots, he shouted forth the chorus:

"I wear a red collar,
  I drank saxteen dollar
Wit' ax handle in my hand!"

Singing made Ax-Handle Ole forget all about the intruder for a moment. It made him feel good all over. He kept stamping his boots. He pulled his pants high around his thick thighs. "Yah, by golly, that's me, all right, Ax-Handle Ole, strongest damn Swede ever come out of Nort' Dakota." Then he noticed Tim. "You still har? Didn't I tell you to get your handcar back down the track?"

To give force to his words, he lunged with arms

wide, apparently expecting that would frighten him to flight. Instead, Tim Chipman shifted his feet and met him with a left jab, half feint, and a solid right smash to the jaw.

It set Ole solidly in the middle of the track. His red hat fell off. His blond hair was jarred over his face. His eyes for just a second looked off focus. Then with a roar he lunged to his feet.

He had the ax handle. He swung it horizontally with a force that would have taken Tim's head off had he not dropped to one knee. He could feel the wind passage of it over his head. Missing, it carried Ole off balance. He was half turned, and Tim, rising, hit him three times. They were beauties, but Ole absorbed them. He took them without blinking.

"Lay off the ax handle!" shouted the black-whiskered one.

"Hah!" said Ole. He did. He tossed the ax handle aside. He took another blow without trying to block it, merely dropping his head, letting it glance off his cheek and ear, and he charged.

Tim tried to meet him and stop him. He might as well have tried to stop the charge of a bull moose. He felt himself being carried back, his weight over Ole's lowered shoulder, his feet clear of the ground. Finally he twisted loose, but the slanting friable earth of the railroad grade was under his feet. It gave way and he went to his knees, his boots half buried in dirt and gravel.

Ole came down on him, using his weight. They rolled and crashed backward into buckbrush that grew beside the bank. Ole came to his feet, dragging Tim by the mackinaw. He swung his fist, the fist short, sticking his elbow out as the fist missed. The elbow hit Tim alongside the head like a club.

The force of the clubbing blow tore the buttons off his mackinaw. He fell. Ole tried to drag him back, but the mackinaw only rolled him. With a twist of his shoulders he got out of it. He was ready to spring to his feet, but Ole was intent on pinning him there. When Ole tried to drop on him, Tim doubled his legs and uncoiled, hitting him in the abdomen with both feet.

Ole was knocked to his feet. His mouth sagged, his eyes stared, he was paralyzed, unable to get his breath. He backed up the grade. His heels caught one of the rails. He sat down. It was Tim's chance. He had been raised in the timber and knew the rules. He had watched many brutal logger fights. He rolled to his feet, ready to follow and swing his boots to the sides of Ole's head. But at the last instant he realized that the black-whiskered man was behind him.

He tried to turn and parry the blow that was coming. A railroad spike hit him on the back of the neck. He was down with rough gravel and the ends of railroad ties under his hands. He knew he had to turn over and protect himself, but his veins seemed weighted by quicksilver. He could not force his muscles to respond. It was like being caught by disaster in a dream with all his muscles frozen. He was hit again and again, but still he clung to a shred of consciousness. He knew when Ole got up and stood over him. He knew when Ole lifted him and slammed him to the ground, and lifted him and slammed him again, and after that he knew only the flittering unreality of nightmares.

Chapter Three

He did not come awake all at once, but slowly, by degrees, through pain and febrile images. He knew he was carried somewhere, he knew there were voices, and a light that pained his eyes.

He wanted to be left alone, he wanted to lie where it was cool and dark, he wanted to lie still without making the slightest movement, for then the pain in his neck and head would diminish to almost nothing.

It seemed that he slept for hours, although perhaps it was only ten or fifteen minutes. When he awoke he was lying in a bunk on some coarse gray camp blankets. An electric bulb burned at the end of a drop cord lighting a long, brownish, low-ceilinged room.

He turned his head and pain knifed up through his neck, cleaving his skull, making things go black. Slowly vision came back. The room was very large, furnished with wooden chairs, a large pine table, a wall desk and stool, a puncheon bench; at one end was a bookcase heaped full of papers and rolled maps. A fire burned in a horizontal wood stove. The room was too hot. He wondered where he was, and guessed that this was the main office at Talka mill.

Someone was walking. He could not see anyone without turning his head, and that hurt too much. He thought of Ole and of Brunner, but this was no such heavy tread. Then a shadow cut off the electric bulb, and he knew it was a girl.

The light made an aura about her hair, making it look like spun metal. Her face, in shadow, became visible. She was beautiful. She was too beautiful to be real. Laughing to himself, he thought that his dreams had taken a turn for the better. Being slugged into unconsciousness had its recompenses.

"How do you feel?" she asked.

"You're not a dream, then!" he said, having a hard time with his stiff and thickened lips.

"Did you think I was?"

"Yeah, really."

"That's kind of an old line."

"Well, I don't feel very original today."

His lips were bruised so he had to speak without moving them, and she could not understand what he said.

"What?"

He shook his head. "Water."

She went and got it for him. "I'll put some liquor in it if you want."

"No."

Her voice was familiar, the way she moved was familiar, and her face, too. He seemed to remember her, but he pushed the thought away. It wasn't possible.

He drank and looked at her. She was in her early twenties, built the way women should be and not very often are. She wore a wool shirt, a wool skirt that came to her knees, and a pair of high laced boots. The clothes were not exactly selected for allure, but this girl had it. It was the way she curved inside of them. It was the way she moved, as though she didn't mind a man looking at her.

"More?" she asked, taking the glass.

He shook his head.

"Feel better?"

"Yeah."

He sat up and got his feet on the floor. Each time he moved he was blacked out momentarily from pain. He had taken a terrible beating. That black-whiskered one with the spike in his hand. That's what had happened to his neck. And Ole lifting him and hurling him to the ground! Every joint and muscle ached. He passed a hand gently across his face. One side was puffed and raw. The big Swede had given him the hobs, too.

"His goons got to me, didn't they?"

"I'm sorry, but he was only doing his job," she said with a bit of defensive anger.

"*They* were only doing *their* job. You don't think one man did all this. I'd have licked the Swede, but the black one got me from behind."

"I'm sorry," she said, and he decided that she really meant it.

"Where am I?"

"This is the company house."

"Talka?"

She nodded.

He kept staring at her and it made her uncomfortable. "Don't move. Just stand there."

"Why?"

"I was wondering where I'd seen you before."

"I'm Lynne Tilton."

He remembered her. Lynne Tilton, old Swiftwater Tilton's daughter. Swiftwater—he was the founder of the Swiftwater Lumber Company. The Tiltons used to live in one of those big, white, two-story houses on the hill in Prince Albert. The Tiltons had eaten from bone china and sterling on a linen-covered table, while the Chipmans had been a rough crowd, living in a log house with an outside privy. Beans, moose meat, and baking-powder biscuits on an oilcloth-covered table had been old Pat's idea of something pretty fancy. As a result Tim had always felt uncomfortable and clumsy in her presence. But that had been in his prep-school days, he a senior and she just starting in. He had been around a little since then. He felt a trifle less big-footed, but damn it, she was still beautiful.

"I'm Tim Chipman," he said.

"I thought so," she said, and she paled a little.

"*You* didn't know me. *Burgess* didn't know me."

"Your face is so swollen."

"Who hired that big Swede? Not Swiftwater. Say, what are you doing here? I thought this was Talka property."

"We're sort of—in together."

He didn't like it. "Oh," he said. He kept rubbing his jaw. His lips functioned better now, but they were cut inside and the cuts tasted brassy. "Funny, I thought us Chipmans built that rail line. Thought it went to Chipman. In fact, it's against the law to block it off without a court order, and I'd imagine I could take this piece of beefsteak I please to call a face into court and—"

"It wasn't my fault!"

"No."

"It all boils down to the fact that the road had been falling apart and Chipman wouldn't pay its share in fixing it up, so Swiftwater and Talka went ahead with the job, since they own two-thirds of the stock."

"And closed the line at their north boundary."

"It isn't safe."

"You're saying all this happened to me for my own good?"

"Don't joke. I'm sorry. I'm sorry about everything."
And she started to cry.

"Now, kid. I was just shooting my gab. I didn't mean a thing."

"It was so awful, when you were on your way up there after—Clay. You didn't even get here in time to see him."

At first he thought they had taken him out on the plane, but with a sick shock it came to him that Clay was dead.

"What about Clay?"

"Didn't you know?" She stopped crying. She stared at him. She looked frightened.

"No."

"He's dead. I thought of course you knew."

"Burgess told me he was hurt. When did he die?"

"Three days ago. You said you talked to Burgess."

"He was afraid to tell me, I suppose. Maybe he wanted me to be surprised. Maybe he was afraid he'd say something that Brunner would call a mistake."

"What do you mean?"

"Forget it. Forget it, kid. How'd it happen?"

"They found him along one of the old skid roads. He'd crawled into the brush, I guess, or he'd been dragged in there. He'd been in a fight or something. His skull had been fractured. The doctor flew over from Chinook. He was going to fly him out to the hospital, but he died while they were carrying him."

"Who was it, Ole?"

"What you're really doing," she said with a tight mouth, "is accusing Swiftwater and Talka of murder."

"No, kid, no. *Companies* don't murder. Just the men who run them. But I'm not accusing anybody."

"You mean it was Croft?"

"I hadn't thought it through that far. I don't suppose I will for a while. Maybe he had trouble with one of the boys up there. We haven't been able to hire the best men lately, you know. But I'll find out. Sometime I will, and I won't accuse anybody."

"It wasn't Croft. Please believe me."

"O. K., so it wasn't."

He had been fond of Clay, but he hadn't seen him for a long time, and that made it easier to take. Anger was there, and suspicion, but they had settled cold and deep, and his face did not show it. He stood up, not minding the pain any more. His face looked lean and hollow-cheeked with the bone structure of his jaw and forehead sharply marked by the oblique rays of the electric bulb. He seemed very tall beneath the low ceiling.

"How about the law? Mountie been up there?"

"Constable Andrews from Chinook was there with the doctor."

"Sorry if I said anything I shouldn't have. It knocked my pins from under me." He grinned and said, "I could stand a jolt of that liquor now."

Chapter Four

IT HAD GROWN DARK OUTSIDE. There was a slight coating of mist on the windows, and Tim Chipman smeared it away with the heel of his hand to look out. He could see the mill and the yard lighted by floods. A truck was just coming around with its dual wheels deep in the rutted road, its load consisting of three thick log segments.

"Big sticks," he said. "Where are you timbering now?"

"Forney Ridge."

"That was all Douglas fir."

"Yes."

He remembered back to the days when not one of the big outfits would touch those Douglas stands, considering the fir unfit for anything but firewood, almost in a class with larch and poplar, but the timber market had changed. Gone were the times when the only saw log worth taking was white pine.

He sat with his second drink, a long one with hot water from the teakettle, and they talked about old friends and the days when they were both in school at Prince Albert. And he answered her questions about his years since then, his years in college and his seasons with the Black Hawks.

He felt a stir of draft and knew that a door had opened. He heard it click shut and a sound of boots in a passageway. He knew by glancing at Lynne's face who it would be.

Croft Brunner came to a stop in the door. He evidently believed himself to be beyond their sight. He stood for several seconds, a shadowy, big form in the reflection of the electric bulb. He was shorter and broader than Tim Chipman. They probably weighed about the same, but Brunner's thickness of body made him look heavier. He was in his middle thirties.

He saw them looking at him then and turned to take off his hat and mackinaw, which he hung carefully, almost fastidiously, on some caribou antlers that served as a coat tree. Then he came inside smoothing his hair down.

"Well, Chipman!" he said. "I heard, I heard, and I'm sorry."

He had a direct seriousness that made his words believable. He came on with his right hand extended. They shook hands. He had a strong grip. Everything about him showed strength, his walk, his movements, his face. Even Tim Chipman had to admit that he was good-looking. Perhaps his mouth was too small for his jaw, and his eyes too pale. And years before he had been struck by a peavey that had split the skin near his right eye, giving it a puckery scar that sometimes made him seem calculating. Or maybe it was just that Tim, in his loyal Chipman manner, hated his yellow guts.

Anyway, they shook hands.

It occurred to Tim that he didn't know whether Brunner meant he was sorry about Clay or about the beating his thugs had given him.

"We live and die," said Tim, thinking that would take care of either.

"Yes, Clay! A great fellow. His kind carved it out of the wilderness and left it here for us, Tim, and there aren't many of them left. Oh, I know we had our differences, and he didn't like me, but I never denied that it was Clay and your dad who got me into the business."

Tim smiled to himself, thinking about those logs Brunner had pirated off the Rouge River drive.

"I never beat you Chipmans out of a toothpick," Brunner said pleasantly, "but your dad and Clay did teach me the business. So when I learned he was having a hard time up there, I offered to help him out. I did, I swear to God I did, and Lynne will back me up. I want you to know that, Tim. I want you to believe me. The country's big enough for all of us, Tim. It always was, and it still is."

Brunner looked him straight in his eyes when he said it, the pucker in his right eyelid making it seem just a little bit appraising. Then he shrugged, indicating that that phase of their conversation was at an end. He turned and walked to the sideboard. He had a way of showing off the power of his legs. He wore rough wool, there was muck and sawdust ground into his clothes, he courted the appearance of a timber stiff, but nobody would ever have mistaken him for one. There was something in every move he made that stamped him as the big tyee.

He got the whisky bottle and glanced at it. It was only

a brief shift of his eyes, but Tim knew he'd noticed the drink that was gone. Brunner was not stingy, but he kept tabs on the things that were his. He came back with the bottle, saying, "What's this I hear about you having an argument with Ax-Handle Ole?"

"That dirty—"

"Now, Tim. Now, now. We know what those boys are like. What they always have been. And you swung at Ole first."

"I was taken from behind by one of your goons with a railroad spike."

"Well." He did not call Tim a liar, but the inference was there. And he smiled without taking the cut of it away.

Anger flowed through Tim's body, but he managed to control the outward signs of it.

Tim said, "Burgess telephoned you that I was coming, didn't he?"

"Have a drink, Tim."

"No, let's settle this. Burgess called you, and you sent those goons up there to stop me."

"The barricade has been there for weeks."

"My father and uncle built that line up there, and no big-footed Swede with an ax handle is going to stop me from going through."

"Don't make an issue of it."

"Why?"

He glanced at Lynne. "This isn't the place."

"It suits me."

She cried, "No, Croft! Not tonight!"

What she meant was plain enough: She didn't want Brunner to tangle with him on the heels of the bad news about Clay.

"Sure, girl," Brunner said. He patted her arm. There was a possessiveness in his manner that made Tim feel sick and sweaty. It was as if he had taken her over together with the Swiftwater Company. It shouldn't have made any difference, he had forgotten her existence until a few minutes ago, but he didn't want her belonging to Croft Brunner.

"That's right, Tim," Brunner said. "If we have to have it rough, this isn't the time or place. Now let's have that drink."

"All right."

Brunner poured him a stiff slug, but only a few drops for himself. "Happy days," he said, and they drank. "How long you been gone now, Tim?"

"Seven years."

"School, professional hockey. McCabe was in Montreal and saw you play there. You were with the Black Hawks."

"Yes."

"I never played hockey. I never went to school, either. Not past the seventh grade. You think you've had it tough, Tim? You never had it tough at all. Not like me. I was raised in a shack down in Oregon. My mother died when I was ten, and one day my old man just never came home. I found out he'd run off with a biscuit shooter at the hotel. I was going to sell the house—a fellow offered me seventy dollars for it—and a cheap, two-bit lawyer beat me out of it. Me just a kid. Can you imagine a man like that? I hit the road. Know how I started out in the timber business? As flunky for the crumb boss. That was down in McCloud. The big tyee was a Britisher by the name of Dillingham. He had graduated from a German university and when he came there he didn't know the difference between bull pine and Sitka spruce, but he knew some other things. He could stand there with his slide rule and figure more timber in five minutes than our log boss could cipher out with a pencil and paper all winter. The timber stiffs all laughed at him behind his back, but just the same he was the one living in the big house. That's when I made up my mind I'd never be just a strong-armed stiff in a pair of tin pants. I decided I'd learn something. I used to go up there and flunky around the kitchen. Every once in a while I'd swipe one of his books, and after everybody was in their bunks I'd read it. Then I'd take it back and swipe another. I got by on five hours' sleep, and I still do. It wasn't so easy at first. Sometimes I'd fall asleep in the kitchen and the crumb boss would take it out of my hide with a skillet. Nobody ever fed it to me out of a Wedgwood dish. But I got it."

Tim wondered if he was talking for the girl's benefit, and decided he wasn't. He was talking more for himself, proving to himself that he was better than a Chipman.

He went on. "Yes, I got it the hard way, Tim. I started from nothing and made it in a tough game. Now you're starting. You'll find out how rough it is. Rougher than those Black Hawks. You had a sample of it up there on the tracks. Sure, I'm sorry the boys had to rough you up and didn't know when to quit, but that's the kind of business we're in. You shouldn't hold it against anybody."

"I know the timber business. I was raised here, remember?"

"I wonder if you do know it. After you've picked up the pieces of the Chipman outfit and put it back together again, and then when you hold it together and make money, *then* you'll know the timber business."

"Like you did Talka."

"Sure, like I did Talka. When I bought the company it was held together by haywire and mortgages. And it was tough times then, at the tail end of the depression, and then the war making it impossible to get a piece of machinery anywhere. But I did it. I made it pay." He became serious and sympathetic. "It'll be tougher for you, Tim. Things get bigger every year. You have to have more capital to operate. Now the unions are raising hell. You'll need more than I did. And that layout that Clay has left you!" He waved a hand toward the upcountry. "It'll be a stone around your neck. Everything gone to hell, and what's left saddled with mortgages. I'm telling you, Tim, you'd be better off if there was nothing at all and you could just start out with an ax."

"I'd start out with an ax if somebody'd put all the clear white pine back."

"Yes." Mention of white pine brought a sharp, sidelong look from Brunner's eyes. "What I was getting at, nobody would take it as a sign of weakness if you just sold out for what you could get and started fresh somewhere else."

"I'll stay."

Brunner accepted the challenge with a smile at the edges of his teeth. "The confidence of youth!"

"I'll stay."

"No railroad, you know. That'll make it tough."

"Now we're back to that again! That line is one-third Chipman."

"Granted. Provided you pay the assessment on your stock."

"How much is that?"

"I don't know. Maybe Clay sold some of it. If not, eleven thousand."

"That's what you had trouble with Clay about!"

"Now, wait! Don't get some crazy idea in your head that I was behind what happened to him." He paced the room and stood with his powerful legs set wide, back to the stove, arms clasped behind him. "You wouldn't have known your uncle the last couple of years, Tim. He got sort of—queer. He thought everybody was trying to get him from behind. You know how Chipman, Talka, and Swiftwater always worked, never paying much attention to boundary lines. If we had to cross into another man's territory to yard some logs, we did it. I needed to use three miles of road on his cut-over treaty lands to log that North Boundary tract of mine, and he stopped me with a gang of men who weren't even loggers. They were toughs he hired from one of those Prince Albert saloons."

"Fellows like Ax-Handle Ole?"

The thrust angered him. "I'm trying to be decent about this, Chipman!"

Tim laughed. He looked around for his hat. Lynne handed it to him. "My handcar still up there?"

"No."

"Where is it?"

"Down at the shed. I told them to take it there. It's railroad property."

"You mean you'd let me walk rather than—"

"Rather than go through the barricade, yes!"

"Oh, Croft!" said Lynne.

"It's a matter of principle," he said to her. "It's just business. The barricade stays up until the assessment is paid on that Chipman block of stock." He turned back to Tim. "No, you don't need to walk. I'll send you up there in a jeep. Damn it, I'll have Ole carry you up there on his back. But you're not taking the handcar through."

"I'll walk. The exercise will be good for me. It looks like I'll need to be in pretty good shape. Signs point toward a tough winter."

"Croft!" she said. "Don't let him. Send for the jeep."

"No, I really meant it," Tim said. "I'd like the walk. I'll get there before midnight, and it'll give me some time to think things over."

He found his plunder bag and suitcase in the hall. She

walked ahead and opened the door. Brunner waved
without moving. At the door she said, "Well, good night,
Tim. I'm sure everything will work out all right."

"Sure, kid, sure."

What a nice voice she has, he thought as he stood on
the porch, letting his eyes grow accustomed to the early
darkness. What a sweet kid! He wondered if she had
made any promises to Brunner. She had been wearing no
ring, but the way he treated her, he seemed to feel as if
he owned her.

There was a company store or wangan house close by.
Beyond were the cabins and shacks where the mill fami-
lies lived, and farther on were the bunkhouses. Men were
seated along the store platform. They had been talking,
and now they stopped. Without appearing to, they
watched him.

He went down the steps. The corduroy led him past
them. He nodded and spoke and got a muttered response. He was ready to go on by when Ax-Handle Ole
came outside the store. Ole saw him and came to a stop.
He was munching Cracker Jack. He kept munching it.
The ax handle was under his left arm. He held it there
while his left hand held the box of Cracker Jack.

Tim knew it was best to keep going, but he didn't. He
stopped and put his suitcase and war bag down. He
grinned at Ole, who still ponderously munched the
Cracker Jack. The left side of Ole's face was puffed out,
and he had a mouse on his eye, but aside from that he
seemed to be in good shape.

"I got to give you credit, Ole," Tim said. "You're a
real strong fellow."

Ole was guarded and suspicious. "Yah?"

"You gave me a real lesson this afternoon. I thought
you were just strong. I didn't think you'd be a real fighting man."

"Ho-ho!" said Ole.

"One thing about me, I'm a good loser, and you sure
did lick me. I thought you'd have a good punch, that
didn't surprise me—what surprised me was your being so
quick."

"Ha-ha! By golly, I quick feller, all right." He finished
the Cracker Jack and threw the box away. He snapped
his suspenders. "Yah, I been in some geud fights. Nobody
teaching tricks to Ole. I fought in Nort' Dakota, in

Coeur d'Alene, all over hell. Been halibut trooler in Pacific Ocean. Fight all kind of feller. Can't teach Ole many new tricks, I tell you that."

"Come here, Ole. Let's see if you know this one."

He was suspicious. "Yah?"

"It's that ax handle. Somebody might take it away from you and beat you over the skull with it."

"Ho-ho!" shouted Ole, stamping his hobs. "You tank you could take ax handle away from Ole, you're crazy."

"Come along."

"Hah!"

"Go ahead, Ole!" someone urged him.

Ole looked around at the audience, which had been growing as truck drivers and millhands came off shift.

"O. K., har's ax handle!" and he stepped forward, holding it out rigidly in an arm solid as an oak beam.

Tim grabbed hold of the ax handle and jerked it back and forth, this way and that; then he let go. A grin spread across Ole's vast face.

"Ho-ho!" shouted Ole. "I knew geud Norsk girl in Fargo, Nort' Dakota, one time was stronger than *that!*"

The ax handle was still out, perpendicular to the pole sidewalk, but Ole for the moment had relaxed his caution. Tim seized it with both hands and rammed forward.

Force coming in that direction put Ole off balance. He had to stagger half a step, and that was enough. Quick as a springing cougar, Tim Chipman placed both feet against Ole's groin and fell backward, pulling him by the ax handle.

Ole plunged head forward. Tim twisted over. He caught his weight with one shoulder on the walk, both hands still gripping the handle. He rammed the ax end of the handle in a crack between the poles. The handle for an instant was like a vaulting pole, carrying Ole's weight. Then the sidewalk stopped it and tore it from his fingers. He sailed on, a lunging, sprawling, Gargantuan figure, and lay spread-eagled on his face.

Tim jerked the handle free and stood with it in two hands like a ball bat. He waited for Ole to get up. It took the big fellow a while. One side of his face was full of splinters and starting to bleed. He looked around, baffled. Then his eyes focused on Tim and he was ready to start forward, but the ax handle dissuaded him.

"Come on," said Tim. "I'll show you the rest of it. I said somebody would beat you over the skull with it, didn't I?"

Ole might have accepted the challenge, but Brunner, in the door of the company house, shouted, "Ole!"

Ole filled himself with a deep, deep breath. He turned slowly as Brunner walked toward him along the corduroy.

"It'd serve you right if somebody did cave your head in," he said to Ole. And to Tim, "That was a good trick, Chipman. Now if you're that good at arithmetic, maybe you'll get somewhere in the lumber business."

Tim tossed the ax handle aside and again hoisted his suitcase and war bag. "I'll study up on it. You can't tell, maybe I'll end by figuring you right out of the country."

Brunner laughed until there were tears to wipe away from the corners of his eyes. "Good boy! If there's one thing I like to see, it's a man with spirit."

Chapter Five

Tim walked down the railroad track. It was farther to the barricade than he had supposed. It was very dark with the bank rising on both sides, the moon not up, and mist covering the stars.

He sensed someone ahead of him, or perhaps there had been a sound. Watching, tensely alert now, he saw the deeper shadow of the barricade and the reflection of metal. Someone was there with a rifle.

There were two men, but neither had been there that afternoon. They stood quietly, leaning against the barricade, watching him.

"Hello," he said, and they answered him.

He walked by. It was a relief when he felt darkness covering him, and a greater relief when a bend in the tracks hid him from view.

The tracks guided him. It was so dark now, with forest bowering over the tracks, that he sometimes could not see the next step ahead. There was no sound except for his own walking and breathing.

The moon rose misty and diffused, and mist kept coming more heavily. The air felt sharply cold with a tooth of wind, and moisture commenced to crystallize from the atmosphere and strike him. He pulled his hat down and walked against it. After an hour each tie became outlined in white that glowed like phosphorescence in the dark. Cold made his bruised face hurt.

At last the forest opened, and he could see the camp of Chipman dimly in front of him. After seven years, this was home.

He felt both fulfillment and disappointment. It was less than he had remembered it. It was the same, but it seemed to be on a smaller scale. The old mill buildings were dark and shrunken. Everything seemed to have moved closer to the earth, and there was an abandoned look about it. It was the darkness, he supposed, and the mist, and the thin coating of snow that made things blend with the earth. Lights burned in a couple of windows. One was a cabin, the other the frame building where the woods boss, Steve Riika, lived and had his office. He had to smile when he thought of Steve's office.

He had a large room just devoted to that; in the middle of the room was a roll-top desk that he had bought secondhand at Kamloops, and on the desk were a thick pencil tablet and some pencils. "Well, I think I'll go work on my books," Steve would say almost every night after grub, and nobody would even hint a smile until he was far out of the room.

Like Talka camp, Chipman also had a large frame company building, bunkhouses, a wangan shack, cache houses. All this stood on high ground, so as to be well away from the spring floods. Only slightly lower were the mill and the railroad sidings. The river was a strip of tarnished metal a quarter mile away.

A billow of sparks rose from Steve's chimney, indicating that someone had added wood to the fire.

He started down a short-cut path and he was halted by the sharp click of a gun hammer being drawn to cock.

"Hello!" Tim said into the shadow beneath some cedar trees.

"Stay there!" a strange voice said after a second of hesitation. "Who are you?"

"I'm Tim Chipman."

"Clay's nephew?"

"Yes."

He could make out the man now climbing slowly through rock and forest litter, a rather slight figure with a rifle across his arm. There was nothing familiar about him.

"Got a match?" the man asked.

"Yeah."

"Light it."

He thought at first he wanted to light a smoke; then he knew that the fellow wanted to see his face.

He found a match, lit it, and held it until it burned down. "I just came up from the Landing."

"What happened to you? You look like you'd had a run-in with a bulldozer."

"Oh." He laughed. "Next thing to it. I met Ax-Handle Ole."

"Well, I guess you're Chipman, all right. Steve has been expecting you."

They walked together to Steve's office. The fellow was about twenty-one, slim, and small-faced. His name was George Holman. "One of the Babish Lake Holmans," he said. He laughed and added, "Holmans are thicker than muskrats in that country."

"They buried my uncle, of course?"

"Couple days ago. I didn't mean anything, joking like that. I suppose it sounded—"

"Oh, forget it. Of course not." He nodded at the gun. "That thing necessary?"

"You're damn right it is! You know what happened to Clay."

"Who did it?"

"I don't know. Nobody *knows*."

"Brunner?"

"Somebody ought to go down there and kill him. That's what they ought to do. They should take a gun—"

"Well, don't you try it."

"They ain't through. You're liable to be the next."

He felt of his bruised face and remarked that he damned near was.

Steve heard their voices and came to the door. He was a broad, gray-grizzled figure with the light behind him, trying to see through the dark.

"George?" he said. "That you, George? Somebody with you?"

"Steve!" said Tim.

"Tim! That you, Tim? I was afraid you didn't get my message. I was afraid—"

"I got it, Steve," he said, and coming forward with long strides he put his arm around the old man's shoulders. "I'd have chartered a plane in here if I'd known—"

"You wouldn't have got here in time, anyhow. He was dead already when I come back after sending the wire. Had to walk all the way to Vermilion to use the telephone. And that damned Burgess—"

"Sure, Steve. I know." They went inside and closed the door. The office looked exactly the same. A coal-oil lamp burned on a suspension chain above the old roll-top desk. The desk was open, and Steve had been making notations in Finnish on his pencil tablet. A fire in a wood stove was burning with a friendly roar. "Who was it?"

"Hah?"

"Who killed Clay?"

"I doon know," Steve said with his Finlander accent, shaking his head. "I doon know, that's the truth."

"You *know!*"

"Not for sure. You sit down. You Chipmans get awful mad, do crazy things. You sit down and I'll make you a cup of instant coffee. I'll even put a little shot of moose milk in it. You promise me you won't do nothing until after you sleep."

"Brunner, wasn't it?" There was a raw edge to his voice.

"Maybe. They been fighting two-three year. Oh, not like old days. Worse. They were out to kill each other sure. One night Clay got his rifle, that old forty-five-ninety. You hit a moose with that old gun, you'd have nothing but horns and tail."

"Yeah?"

"Well, he was going down there and shoot him. Yah, Brunner. He said it was one kill the other, sooner or later. Now I wish he had!"

Tim sat down and dropped his hat and mackinaw on the floor. He was tired, and that beating hadn't helped. He sat rubbing the back of his neck. He didn't agree with Steve. He didn't think Clay should have taken the gun to him. Well, Steve was just talking. Murder was a terrible thing to have to live with. Tim had often thought he'd rather be killed himself than live out his years with killing on his conscience. He was glad Clay didn't have it on *his* conscience. Or maybe his life outside had softened him up.

"Brunner said Clay was getting sort of crazy."

"You talk to Brunner?" Steve was straight and furious with his fists doubled.

He touched his face. "I talked with him."

"You fight with him?"

"Ole."

"What happened?"

"Ole just let me know I couldn't take a handcar through the barricade. It wasn't anything. I stuck my chin out."

"You talked to Brunner!"

"He said he had nothing to do with it. He said it was somebody here in the camp. Oh, I guess he didn't *say* it. He meant it."

"He's a dirty liar! That is what he told the mounted policeman, too."

"Did the mountie believe it?"

"I don't know. Maybe halfway, yes."

"Take it easy now, Steve. Just sit down here and tell me about Clay."

Steve sat down. He shook his big, rounded shoulders in a laugh, saying, "Here I say you Chipmans get awful mad and do crazy things, and listen to me!" Steve was in his sixties, very thick through, but without fat. His gray hair was so thick it stood stiffly out in locks that defied combing, if he ever tried. He had intensely blue eyes that made a pleasing contrast with his tanned skin. Like many of his race, he had small, almost womanish features.

"They been fighting, let's see, well, about year and a half now. I know pretty soon somebody get killed. Brunner close the railroad, Clay chase his loggers off North Boundary tract. Brunner send goons through with his trucks, Clay go up and blast out the road. What the hell, Clay said, the road's on his land. He can blast any place on his land he wants to. This is against the right-of-way law. All right, says Clay, how about the railroad right-of-way? Then three or four weeks ago Brunner came down here and tried to buy Clay out. Oh, he's got plenty of guts, that Brunner. Walked right up here all alone while that Holman kid was standing there with his rifle not even batting an eye."

"What'd he want to buy? The whole outfit?"

"Oh, sure. But he had quite a proposition. I think Clay was maybe crazy for not taking that proposition. He offered sixty-seventy thousand dollars for all our timber north of Granite Knob Mountain, but Clay told him to go to hell. I think Clay was crazy to tell him to go to hell. Of course, it was because it was Brunner. If anybody else had made that offer, he would have taken it like that!"

"What did Brunner want with that timber?"

"I don't know. You know how Brunner is, always buying crazy timber all over."

It always looked crazy and ended up smart.

Guessing what was on his mind, Steve said, "Brunner, he's in with the devil. Plain lucky. He'd fall in a mine shaft and come out with his hands full of gold."

"Yeah. I think the first thing I'll do is cruise that timber north of Granite Knob."

They talked until dawn, Steve telling how, after turn-

ing down Brunner's proposition, Clay had gone to Nokewin Lake to look at some Douglas fir he was logging.
They had expected him back all day Thursday. On Fri-
day, one of the teamsters found him three miles out on
the west road, unconscious from a beating around the
head and shoulders. He had never regained consciousness.

Tim went over the books. An average of twenty men
had been kept on the payroll. No paydays had been
missed. Clay had been eking out his expenses by logging
some Douglas fir on the steep slopes of Nokewin Lake,
from where it could be rafted to a mill at Silver Junction
on the Canadian National. Supplies he brought up from
there by bateau, and cross-country by truck, although the
road was impassable in the early summer because of
muck, and in winter because of deep snow. His alternate
route was across the Granite Knob by cat and trailer, although that, too, was blocked by snow during January,
February, and March. With the rail line blocked, and
apparently with the legal right to do it, Brunner could
sit tight and wait.

Tim slept late in the morning. He awakened and visited the camp cemetery, where Clay was buried beside
the other Chipmans, his father, his uncle Billy, who had
died forty years ago, and his mother, whom he could
scarcely remember. Then he went through all the buildings, inspected the books, and ended with all the old
company survey maps spread out on a large table in
Clay's office.

The country north of Granite Knob especially interested him. It was a wild area, removed from roads and
water transportation except for Mad River, a stream that
at most seasons was insufficient for log drives, and at all
times too swift for rafting. Once when he was fourteen or
fifteen, Jim Stimak, a timber cruiser, had taken him
through there, but he could remember little except that
the scenery was spectacular, and that some of the streams
on the southern slope were teeming with arctic trout.

But as he thought far back, he had a picture memory
of something else. He could remember himself lying on
his back, half asleep, waiting for Stimak to return, looking at blue sky far, far above through the tops of lofty
pines—the white pine giants of the northern forest.

"There's white pine up there, big stuff," he said to

Steve Riika that night at the table as the Chinese cook brought their grub to them.

"Sure. Plenty damn big white pine. Some on the Natoose, some on McKenna Creek. Some farther on . at Wheelbarrow Gulch, where they used to have the gold diggings. Some even at Chilkao. But it would cost two dollars to get each dollar's worth out."

Tim put the maps in a carrying case, made a wolf bindle for himself, and cruised his timber. He spent ten days making a general inspection of the Chipman holdings. He saw some vast areas of timber, but much of it was alpine, only a small percentage ready for the saw. There was a small amount that could be successfully logged and yarded in the foreseeable future, but none, aside from the Nokewin Lake fir, that could reach market without using the railroad.

He was back at headquarters camp taking a bath, standing shin-deep in a tub of water heated on the stove, when he heard the sharp impulse of a two-cylinder engine, and looking through the smoky window he saw a railroad speeder come up the track from the direction of Talka. There were six men on it, and one of them was Croft Brunner.

Chapter Six

TIM CHIPMAN quickly dried himself and dressed and stepped outside. Brunner and a second man had been stopped by Hilde Vodal, a sawyer who doubled as a watchman now that the mill was shut down.

"All right, Hilde!" Tim called, and Hilde put his rifle down.

Brunner waved to Tim and spoke, and the other man spoke, too. It was only after they'd covered a hundred yards of the distance that Tim recognized him as Swiftwater Tilton.

When Tim attended high school at Prince Albert, Tilton was the town's leading citizen. Although he held no public office, no civic enterprise was ever undertaken without consulting him. He was a reserved, austere man, very thin and straight, with the ways of a retired army officer, which he was not. Tilton had made the mistake of maintaining his level of operations during the depression, however, with the result that he faced a receivership, and would have failed altogether if Brunner had not bought up enough of his outstanding paper to rescue him.

Failure, Tim could see, had left its mark on Tilton. He no longer had his erect, crisp manner. He had put on some soft weight, his skin was pink and pouchy, he even needed a shave.

"Remember him, Mr. Tilton?" Brunner asked, waving at Tim.

"Well, Tim!" Tilton cried. No hint of his old austere manner remained. He seemed pitifully to want Tim to remember him. His hand felt peculiarly lifeless when they shook hands. He smelled of liquor. Not the sharp whisky odor of one who had just taken a drink, but the stale hint of saturation.

Swiftwater started to say how badly he felt about Clay, and Tim cut him off as soon as possible to talk about things at Prince Albert, about Lynne, his other daughter, Florence, now married to a doctor in Seattle, and his son, Norbert, who was a construction engineer in Montreal. All the while Brunner said little but followed along beside Tilton, his eyes shrewdly taking in every feature of the camp without seeming to. There was not much now that had not been there when he was log boss for Chipman, but he could compare its value then with its value now.

"We gave you a bad home-coming, very bad," Swiftwater was saying with anguish, and Brunner cut him off.

"That's all water over the falls."

Assuming that they wanted to talk business of some nature, Tim led them inside the office.

"Yes, yes, of course," Tilton kept saying as his eyes shifted around the room, apparently in the hope that Tim would produce a bottle, but it was a vain hope. There wasn't a drop Tim knew of except the bottle Steve kept for medicine.

Tim seated them and asked them what they wanted.

"Business," said Brunner with his big, solid legs crossed. "I was up here a while ago and made an offer to Clay. He turned it down. It was fair, so I'll make the same offer to you. I'll pay you seventy thousand dollars for the timber you control north of the Granite Knobs. That will leave you in possession of all that you're logging now except that section above Nokewin Lake. Furthermore, I'll open the railroad and you can have as much time as you need to meet the stock assessment, though with that seventy thousand it shouldn't be any worry. Now there's one *hell* of a proposition!"

It made Tim Chipman feel considerably less bankrupt to hear someone say seventy thousand dollars. The proposition was a good one, all right. But Brunner wasn't the sort of fellow who went around making good propositions.

Brunner followed him with his eyes. He seemed to be trying to read Tim's mind. "Well, isn't it?"

"You're right. That's a lot of money."

"Cash."

"I wouldn't feel good about it if I robbed you."

Brunner laughed, squeaking back in the chair, and said, "The hell you wouldn't! You'd send me over the hill without a shawl if you had the chance, and we both know it."

"What's up there, gold?"

"You don't own the mineral rights, so—"

"I was joking."

"The truth, Tim—I buy for the future. I have a policy

of buying two sections of marginal and submarginal timber land for every section I log off. It gives a corporation
a solid structure, a permanence. In the mining business
they have a saying, 'The waste of today is the ore of
tomorrow.' And so we see those big outfits like Sunshine
and Anaconda buying big, low-grade deposits that
couldn't possibly be worked under today's conditions,
just laying them away, their faith in the technical devel-
opments of the future."

Tim was thinking that he'd certainly got his money's
worth from his correspondence course in business English.

"I understand that," said Tim. "You should have
offered me thirty thousand. That would about pay off
my quick bills. But seventy thousand! That just makes
a man have delusions of opulence."

"Lynne doesn't like what's been going on. This—
fighting. This gossip that I was responsible for what happened to Clay. Then you getting it. It *was* an asinine
trick, me putting big Ole up there on the track. She
wants it settled. She wants a genuine settlement between
us so we can conduct our affairs like human beings, before we—" He stopped. "Well, sure, it hasn't been made
public, but Lynne and I are going to be married."

Tim felt hot and cold with the old core of hatred
in him. But he controlled himself. He was like all
Chipmans when he had the black mood about him. His
face would go blank with a high-boned look, and his
voice would be soft as buckskin.

"Let's just stick to business."

With a trace of a sneer Brunner said, "Well, if it
would hurt your conscience to take seventy thousand,
I might be able to shade it a little. How about fifty
thousand?"

With his forefinger Tim stood making figures in the
dust that covered the table. "Now you sound like the
old-time Brunner," he said, grinning. "Now I know
you mean business. But let's leave it at seventy thousand."

"You'll sell?"

"I'd like to see it in writing."

Brunner was prepared for that. Some papers were all
made out. He dropped one copy on the table.

"I'll read it over."

"Go ahead."

"I'm a slow reader. Especially all these parties of the 'first part' and 'to wits.' Give me a week or so."

That evening he read the paper through carefully. It was a perfectly straight agreement for sale and transfer of claim. Arising early next morning, he carried out the old files of the company and doggedly went through correspondence, leases, real-estate transfers for all the years Chipman had been in business. He called in Steve Riika, but all Steve could offer was a repetition that Clay had said something must be wrong.

Later that afternoon, feeling the need of the open air after a day of cobwebs and eyestrain, Tim Chipman set out for Talka camp. Tilton was living there while Brunner's main office was now at Vermilion. He was in hopes he could talk to Swiftwater Tilton alone, and that from the talk something might develop.

Yes, seventy thousand was too much. Even as a grandiose gesture before Lynne, seventy thousand was too much.

Night settled, and with it the usual autumn mist. There was no snow now, a warm afternoon had taken it all, but frost had gathered on the spike heads and metal plates close to the ties, which held rot and dampness. He breathed and he could see his breath. The long cold of northern winter was not far away. Soon he would have to turn his thoughts to supplies—that or he'd have to turn his crew loose for the season.

For winter expenses he had two possibilities. There was this deal with Brunner, or he might collect advance payment from the Garvey Company for the winter's take of Douglas on Nokewin Lake.

Now that he was rested and had the downgrade to help him, the trip seemed shorter than it had the other night, and he came to the barricade unexpectedly soon.

He stood for a time watching. A couple of men were talking. They sounded bored with their job. He had not been seen. He climbed the steep side of the cut at his left, pulling himself by means of scrub spruce, and reached the crest of the knoll that separated the railroad from the river. He found a deer trail and, following it, dropped down on the settlement.

The mill and yard were lighted as before. The door of the wangan opened and closed, and he could hear the clip-clap of hobnailed boots on gravel. A man spoke, and the mechanical sound of a radio came with the re-

peated bursts of laughter of a comedy program. In front
of the wangan house three men were sitting, listening
to the radio through the open window, but the comedy
seemed to sadden them.

No one took notice of Tim as he followed one of the
winding truck roads to the street. He met a sawyer from
the mill, a small man whose clothes smelled slightly
skunklike from spruce.

"Where's Tilton live?" he asked, and the man pointed
toward a two-story white frame building off behind a
fence.

"But I think you'll find him at the company house."

"With Brunner?" Tim asked casually.

"I don't know. I don't think so. I didn't see the speeder
when I came up."

Tim thanked him and headed across to the company
house. Apparently Brunner did his traveling back and
forth by rail, preferring the speeder to a jeep on the
pock-marked road.

The big room was lighted, but its windows were misted
over and he could not see inside. He mounted to the
porch and stood beneath the shelter of the snow shed
to listen. No voices. No sound at all. Whoever was there
was probably alone.

He decided not to knock. He quietly opened the door.
He walked on and looked into the long room. There was
Tilton standing by the fire smoking a pipe. He had
poured a drink of whisky, but it was just sitting there.
He wasn't ready for it. He'd probably had quite a few
already.

"Hello, Mr. Tilton," Tim said.

"Oh!" Tilton jumped and knocked ashes from his pipe
down the front of him. "Oh, Tim! You frightened me."
A coal burned the back of his hand and he brushed it off.
"I didn't hear you knock."

"I'm sorry. I didn't knock."

"Sure. That's all right. I've seen the day in this country
when nobody ever thought of knocking anywhere. You
just walked in and made yourself at home. The old days,
Tim, when your father and I first came. I guess I'm
getting old. I keep thinking about the good days long
past."

"Brunner isn't around?"

"Did you want to see him? He's in Vermilion. Or

maybe even in P.A. He has a plane, you know. It shuttles him around, and he's liable to be anywhere, even in Vancouver or Victoria. Did you want to see him about that timber deal?"

Swiftwater waited. He remembered the whisky and offered Tim a drink, but he shook his head.

"I'm sort of on the water wagon."

"I should be. I drink altogether too much of this stuff. But I guess it doesn't make much difference when you get my age."

"Why does he want that timber? Away up there, remote like that, I can't see . . ."

It made Tilton nervous. He lifted the glass. It was quite full and his fingers, shaking, spilled a third of it. He decided to pour another. Then when his hand showed itself too nervous, he stoppered the bottle and pushed it away. He laughed and there was a bitter note in the sound.

"Croft never was noted for his generosity, that's true, I guess this is a case of a man's reputation following him like a stray dog. Now suppose he really *did* want to change and—"

"Yeah."

"There have been stranger things—and for stranger reasons."

"You mean he wants to act human for Lynne."

"Well." He let the word lie there, casting doubt on everything. For just a second or two Tilton was erect again with that old arrogant gleam in his eyes. "No, I won't lie to you, Chipman. Don't let him know I told you this. Don't let anyone know. It might—" Tim knew he had intended to say something about Lynne. He changed his mind. "Well, just keep it under your hat. Before you sell, there's one thing to look into—the High Chilkao grant, north of the Knobs."

Tim was familiar with the High Chilkao timber, a stand of white pine unrivaled in the North, and it would have been gone long ago except for a stipulation in the original grant to the Fitzhugh Company that none of it could be cut for one hundred years. The restriction had something to do with the old National Parks Railroad scheme, that ridge route and a vista of untouched great pines being one of the tourist attractions, but the automobile had changed people's habits, and the railroad never got beyond the stage of surveyors' stakes. Thirty years before the elder Fitzhugh had thrown it in on a sawmill deal. Other timber in the grant was available for cutting, and a small amount had been yarded in the direction of Chinook, but the High Chilkao white pine still did not know the ax, and thirty years of the hundred still stood between it and the hungry saws of Brunner's mill.

He said, "Well, that would be a long-range proposition. Brunner can start cutting that when he's seventy."

"Yes, but there was an old, old law that Brunner dug up. Did you ever hear of the British Columbian Lands Act that Sir Leonard Tilley shoved through to placate the British Columbian interests after the first failure of the Canadian Pacific Railway? There was a clause in that bill which limited the so-called crown restrictions to fifty years, after which they'd have to be renewed. It was passed to free certain islands along the coasts for the salmon canners, but four timber tracts fell under the scope of the act, too. Two of them were destroyed by the great fire back in 1889. Another is now under the National Parks law. The other is Chilkao, and it's clear. Has been clear for years."

Tim whistled softly. "How much do you suppose it's really worth?"

"To Brunner? It would make his Talka River outfit the biggest north of Chilkoos. To you, I can't see that it'd be worth much of anything."

Tim laughed.

"No, you have no way of logging it. Believe me, all of your trouble hasn't come about through accident. He has you bottled and the cork driven in."

"Even if I paid off my rail-stock assessment?"

"Then he'd find something else."

Tim knew that he would. He sat there wondering why Swiftwater had told him. There was only one answer to that: He had been trapped into the partnership but he was still fundamentally a decent man, and Brunner was not.

"What do you think I should do?"

"Sell." Swiftwater caught the look in his eyes and followed it up. "Yes, sell! Don't be stubborn like Clay."

"And end up in a pine box."

"I wish you hadn't said that."

"Well, I didn't mean it just that way. I know you wouldn't associate yourself with anything like murder."

"Brunner isn't a killer. Neither is that dumb Swede. I'll admit Croft is tough and headstrong. He'll trample people to get his way. But he's not a murderer. No matter what Ole babbled the other night, he's *not*. And Clay did have trouble inside his own camp."

"Steve said—"

"I can't help what Steve said. Clay was tough and he was hard to get along with. Sometimes he was late with his pay checks. The boys got to demanding cash. He thought one fellow was an agitator and fired him. It was some big Polack named Bodonik. Clay jumped him and got him down and put the hobs to him. Well, Bodonik had friends. Mind you, I'm not accusing Bodonik. I don't think he's even in the country. But there were several things like that. Then there was some union trouble."

Tim said, "If there was any union trouble it would be here. Clay was hiring union labor."

He said lamely, "Well, I mean the Independent Loggers' Union."

That was the company union organized to keep the international organization from getting a foothold, and Brunner had moved to close the railroad after Clay allowed the international union to organize his camp.

Tim sensed something more to this angle and followed it up. "If the union had a grudge, it would be with Brunner, not Clay."

"Which union do you mean?"

"Now, Tilton," he said kindly, "you and I both know that the company union never complained of anything more serious than a leak in the privy roof."

"The country was better off before it ever heard of a union. It's a hell of a note when a man can't take the business he's saved and worked for—"

"O.K., I might agree or I might disagree, but I'm not going to argue about it. The way things are going, I may be joining one myself."

"With seventy thousand dollars in your pocket—"

"Yeah. Well, that requires some thinking."

"Take it, Tim. Take it!"

He stood there, scratching his chin.

Swiftwater said, almost pleading, "Take it and buy in

on that new pulp mill in Prince Albert. Pulp is the
future of this country. If you still hate Brunner, then
grow in that business and meet him on your own terms."

"I'll look at that High Chilkao first."

"Sure," said Tilton. "Know who you sounded like
then? Just like old Pat. I don't know why I was foolish
enough to think a Chipman would ever be anything
except a Chipman."

Tim returned to camp, getting there about four A.M.
In the morning he went through the old papers on the
Fitzhugh deal. He wanted to check through with the
company barristers in Vancouver, but the phone wire
had been cut off at Talka. He wouldn't have risked using
it, anyway. Instead he wrote a letter and sent a half-
breed kid over the ridge to Chinook with it. He then
went to Silver Junction for a talk with the Garvey
manager, who was willing to recommend a $20,000 ad-
vance against the winter's cut of Nokewin Lake timber.
It would take a week for the matter to clear the main
office at New Westminster, so Tim returned to Nokewin.
There he inquired about Bodonik and learned that he
was a fink from Prince Albert who had been spying on
the union organization, getting the names of the local
leaders for Brunner's private blacklist. Clay, learning
of it, had approached Bodonik with the words, "I'll tell
you who the organizer is, it's me!" and hit him, to the
delight of all.

The really amusing part of it all, to Tim's mind, was
that Clay had always been anti-union too, up until
the time Brunner started bringing in his finks and scabs.
But after that nothing could be said in Clay's presence
against the union. He would have joined himself had the
rules not prevented it.

Returning to the main camp, he learned that Brunner
had been looking for him the day before. That afternoon
Brunner came again.

"You're hard to find," Brunner said.

"Cruising timber," Tim said offhand.

"Above Granite Knob?"

He nodded.

"What did you see?"

"There's some fine white pine up there. You wouldn't
load three segments of *those* logs in one of your trucks."

"Sure," said Brunner, and laughed. "Chilkao!"

Tim had wanted him to say the word first for fear of getting Swiftwater in trouble. But now the word had been spoken it was all right.

"The only trouble is," said Brunner, "you'll have to wait almost forty years before logging it. And by that time those bunglers in Ottawa will probably renew the restriction."

"Well, I'm checking through with my lawyers on that."

Brunner seemed to flinch. His face darkened. His face looked thinner, and his fists clenched. He spoke through tight lips: "And here I thought I was the only man in the North who knew that restriction had expired!"

Still wanting to protect Tilton, Tim said, "Oh, I made a routine checkup on all my titles."

"Sure. Smart business. Well, so what? What do you plan to do with it?"

"Log it."

"You're a fool, Chipman, or you're bluffing. Yes, sure, you're running your bluff. You're smart enough to know that that timber isn't worth five thousand to anybody but me, because I'm the only one who could possibly log it."

"Then there it'll stand, because you're not going to!"

"No?" Brunner smiled, a process of peeling his lips back, showing his powerful teeth. "You're going to keep it?"

"Yes. Not only will I keep it, but I'll take the timber out of there. It's going to make Chipman. It's going to make us all over again."

"Just like the old days!"

Tim nodded, meeting Brunner's eyes.

"How you going to get those sticks out? Across my land? I'll let you truck across my ground just like Clay let me truck across his."

"Then I'll let 'em rot on the ground and sell the knots for firewood."

"I'll make it eighty thousand. No, I'll go all the way, a hundred thousand dollars."

"No."

Brunner took a deep breath. The bulge of his shoulders relaxed. He even managed a laugh. "All right, Tim. Then I'll get it for nothing."

Chapter Seven

BRUNNER LEFT with a wave and a grin, but he was in a savage humor, and Tim Chipman spent an uneasy twenty-four hours, putting an extra watchman out, but word came to him by way of a half-breed Indian that Brunner had taken off for Prince Albert. It was probable he would go on to Victoria to investigate the legal aspects of the business. Sure, that's how it would be, he thought, breathing easier. Brunner would not get rough until he had exhausted the other possibilities. Next day he called his bosses in to the home camp for a meeting.

It was evening when they were all there—Lars Halseth, Dick Poole, Lefty Johnson, and Steve Riika. They sat, heavy-booted and uncomfortable, in the big room while Tim lit the lamps and tacked a large-scale map on the wall. Then, still not saying anything, he used a piece of charcoal to outline the High Chilkao tract of timber.

"You really think you timber it, hah?" Lars asked, unable any longer to keep silent.

"Somebody say I wouldn't?"

Lars lifted his heavy shoulders and let them fall.

Tim knew that talk had been going around the camp, and he wondered where it had come from. For some reason everyone was talking about the High Chilkao; there was talk, too, that the outfit had gone broke and he'd be unable to meet the payroll.

He had an idea it had been planted by someone working for Brunner.

Halseth packed a lip with snoose and Tim could not help thinking of Ax-Handle Ole, but that was ridiculous. They were both Swedes, that was all; he'd have bet his last dollar that Halseth was loyal.

He sharpened the charcoal and dotted in some roads, old wagon trails as he remembered them, or routes where roads would be possible.

"How well do you know that country back there?" he asked.

It turned out that none of them knew it very well.

"You figure you'll truck out of there?" asked Poole.

"I don't know." Where in hell would I get money to buy the trucks? Tim was thinking, but he didn't say it, not with all that talk about his not being able to meet the next payroll. "I have a couple of ideas. I was in hopes you fellows would have a couple more."

"You could truck it, all right," Poole said. "You could bring it across Granite Knob right through the gap and down here to the head of the rail. Downhill and easy all the way, except for that little climb to the Knob." Then with a significant grin on his face he added, "All you'd have to do then is get Brunner to open the line through to Vermilion."

"Think he won't?"

"I *know* he won't."

"He says I won't meet my next payroll, either."

"Well, I don't know anything about that."

They were having trouble keeping men at Poole's camp, and for that reason Tim singled him out.

"I understand there's somebody down at your camp has been stirring things up with that kind of talk."

Poole didn't like it. He hunched forward, a short, thick man with a jaw that was very broad and thick under the ears. It looked thicker now with the muscles knotted. He chewed and spat at a crack and watched Tim while a flush of anger mounted under his skin.

He said, "Goddamn it, Clay never found cause to complain about the way I ran my camp."

"Don't get on the prod. I just have reason to believe that Brunner has somebody planted in your crew."

"I don't fink around the boys at the bunkhouse. They talk about what they damned please. Maybe they talk about you being flat on your financial behind, I don't know. When you're hiring a man you're always a sonuva-bitch, you know that. The way I am with my crew, they can talk about anything they please just so they turn in a good eight-hour shift." Then he cooled off and said, "Anyhow, I don't think Brunner has anybody staked out at my spread."

"How about you, Lars?"

"Me, I'm the worst troublemaker at *my* camp."

He asked Lefty, too, and changed the subject back to the Chilkao. The problems of logging it were discussed until past midnight, but no decision was possible without a survey, and this he had already decided to make.

In the morning he set out with surveying equipment and supplies for a four-day trip on the backs of two pack horses, taking with him a helper, young George Holman. They followed some miles of old corduroy road that led through cut-over hill country to a cluster of dilapidated cabins where Tim's father had had a winter camp about forty years before. The road petered out and they followed deer trails. They crossed a minor divide and might have reached the edge of the Chilkao before nightfall, but instead Tim chose to turn eastward and camp on the Ouragan, a swift little stream, one of the forks of Mad River.

It snowed during the night, a wet, heavy snow that sagged their little tent and gave forth a dampness that penetrated everything. Their boots were stiff from dampness and cold, and it was a long job in the gray, cloudy morning to get wood burning and to cook breakfast.

They went on. It was wild country here, untouched by the ax. As they traveled, the sun came out, melting the snow except for shaded places high along the ridge. They crossed Granite Knob and doubled back to strike the Chilkao along its western limits.

It was magnificent timber, clean-growing with scarcely any underbrush, the huge trunks rising straight as pillars in a Greek temple. The trees rose from brace roots broader than a man's outflung arms tapering to trunks that grew without a branch to remote heights before their green tops were spread toward the sky.

He left young Holman, telling him to stay behind, and walked by himself through the forest. It was very soft underfoot, the accumulation of centuries. The stillness was remarkable. High, high overhead he could see the sky. The forest had a primeval quality as though it had always existed and always would. It was like being alone in a vast cathedral, and it made him feel lonely and insignificant. It was a disquieting feeling, and yet enjoyable. That was why he had left the kid behind. He liked Holman, but he talked too much. Out in the forest there was seldom any need for a man to say anything. He got to thinking about timbering the tract. Destroying the cathedral, he thought with a little smile. He did not like the thought. Then his better judgment told him that the forest was mature, there was no further growth in it, and there was no destruction in taking out the great trees that had reached old age and letting the young rise in their places.

He spent some hours alone, then he stirred himself
and spent the remainder of that day and all the next
and the one after that making his survey. Snow kept
falling a little each night and melting with the sun.
Winter was not far away. It would take some doing to
log a single stick of the High Chilkao this season.

He staked a mile of road across the ridge. Again he
was on the Vermilion side. Far away, below and to his
left, a thin smudge of smoke marked the position of
Lars Halseth's donkey steam engine, where saw logs were
being yarded in the poor anticipation that someday
the railroad would be reopened to Vermilion. In the
other direction, to his right, the rolling country broke
off in the sudden gulches fronting Mad River Canyon.
The distance there was about nine miles. By a coinci-
dence, that was about the length of rail line that lay
unused between Chipman and the Talka River Company's north boundary.

"Why, sure," he said, grinning at the kid. "We'll log
it like that, won't we?"

"Like how?"

But Tim did not explain to him. The only ones he
explained it to were his bosses, and he wasn't too anxious
to do that, but what the hell—a man had to trust somebody.

It was night, the lamp burning, and he stood before
the big map, roughing in the probable course of the railroad.

"Mad River? That's one hell of a stream." It was
Dick Poole talking. He sat hunched forward, as always,
and he had found the crack in the floor that he liked to
spit through. The floor of the office was all brown
along that crack from all the times Dick had visited
and spat through it. "Ten years ago we took some sticks
down the Mad. That was when Dutch Louie was killed.
Luck there weren't three or four more. Blind luck.
Maybe you'll talk lumberjacks into driving down the
Mad."

Lars said, "Old-time lumberjack drive down plenty
streams worse than the Mad."

"Well, maybe the old-timers did, but this is the
twentieth century and we got a union to contend with.
The Mad doesn't carry enough water. Get her in flood
and she'll take one big wash of timber down, but when

the flood's over and those rock reefs start coming through, I'd hate to drive anything bigger'n a beer keg."

"I'll worry about it, Dick," said Tim Chipman, and there was an edge of anger in his voice, although he tried to hide it.

"O.K., I'm just speaking my mind. What the hell? You're not looking for a bunch of yes men?"

Tim laughed and said he certainly didn't have them.

Poole said, "I'd concede you'd get your timber down the Mad a lot quicker than I'd concede it would ever *reach* the Mad. So you relay the old track along those hill contours. O.K., I know nothing about your transit, I'm no surveyor, but what the hell good a rail line is without rolling stock—"

"I'll get it."

Poole narrowed his eyes significantly. "You'll *take* it."

"I'll think of that when the time comes."

"When is the time?"

"I haven't decided."

"You mean you'll grab an engine and a string of cars, bring 'er up, and then tear up the tracks?"

"You're way ahead of me, Dick. I have a legal angle first."

But he was not fooling Dick Poole. "You have like hell. You got it in your craw to go down there and *take* that engine." The humor of it seemed to appeal to Dick. He laughed. He whacked his leg half a dozen times and cried, "Yow! Twist the tiger's tail. To hell with Brunner. Spit in his eye. Tell me when you're going to do it. I'd like to be cut in on that excitement. It's a good way to get an ax handle between the eyes, but cut me in."

"I'll think it over," said Tim.

Tim did think it over. He knew there was no legal way of getting the rolling stock. One of the trains was his by right, but try to get it! He could not sleep. He lay in his bunk, feeling all the lumps of the old mattress beneath him, looking at the dark underside of the bunk above, and thought it all through. He would have to act quickly. If he even hinted at pulling those rails up, Brunner would be expecting the rest. He rose and started groping toward the bunks where Dick and Lars were spending the night.

"Hello!" Lars said.

"It's me. Tim. I been thinking."

"Yah?"

"Dick was right. We'll have to get that train now."

"Tonight?"

"No, it'll take more planning than that. He has a barricade down there. We'll have to time it, and tear down that barricade and run through. What is this, Monday?"

"Yah."

"We need a couple of days to get set. Three, maybe. How about Thursday night?"

"I tank you crazy."

"Well, this is a crazy man's job."

Dick Poole had not made a sound except to breathe, but Tim felt sure he was awake, listening.

Chapter Eight

THE JOB required trustworthy men. He told Lars to find them. "Trustworthy" to Lars meant Swedes, and that's what he chose, all Swedes and all of them old-timers on the Chipman payroll. Lars dropped around the following evening to give Tim their names.

"I hope you didn't tell 'em too much," Tim said.

"Didn't tell 'em nothing. You don't have to tell a Swede nothing. Just promise a Swede maybe he'll find a geud fight, maybe get paid an extra roll of snoose."

"They might find it when they tear down that barricade."

"How about Winchester guns?"

"No. Take a gun along and somebody will shoot it and we'll have a murder charge on our hands."

"Ax handle, though."

"I wouldn't deprive a Swede of his ax handle."

Lars had a drink of whisky with him and left for his camp. Steve Riika sat around and talked to Tim for a while, then Steve went to bed and Tim was left alone.

He kept wondering where Brunner was.

As a practical matter, Tim wished that Brunner were out of the country, because that might simplify taking the train, but an ornery streak in him made him want Brunner to be there so he could take it right from under his damned nose. *His* nose, and the nose of that big ox, Ax-Handle Ole. Tim rubbed the side of his neck. A muscle or tendon in that region pained him in the morning when he arose, or when he got cold, making him remember Ax-Handle Ole.

Tim was thinking that that was his chief trouble—his ornery streak. That's what caused him to spend so much of his hockey career in the penalty box—his quick-to-boil Chipman blood.

He made a vow not to lose his temper. Cool and thoughtful, that would be him from here out. Timber off that High Chilkao, float the logs out, put the old Chipman Lumber Company back into business. That was the way to hurt Brunner. By the gods, that would hurt Brunner worse than breaking his lousy neck.

He did not feel like going to bed. He was lonesome

and restless. He decided to sneak down toward Talka just to see if Brunner *was* there.

Murray Mahon was standing guard up by the tracks.

"Taking a little walk," Tim said to him. "How long will you be on guard?"

"Midnight."

"Who relieves you?"

"Porky."

"Tell him not to shoot me on my way in. I'll warn him when I'm coming."

He walked down the tracks. He wondered why the hell he kept those kids on guard. What if they killed somebody? What would that solve? Yet he couldn't let the place stand without a sentry. That gang of wolves Brunner hired might come up here and burn him out. Especially if he succeeded in getting that train.

The quiet was disturbed only by the sound of his boots on the ties, by the distant howling of wolves and the yapping of coyotes.

Walking in the cold air glazed his mind and he was jolted awake, almost as if from a dream, when he realized that someone was coming toward him between the tracks.

He moved quietly down the grade, found the shadow of some scrub spruce, and waited. Whoever it was had not seen him. A small figure, coming at a steady walk; a boy, he thought. Then with surprise that set his pulse racing he realized it was Lynne Tilton.

"Lynne!"

She was almost opposite him. She stopped suddenly and there was a gun in her hands, a revolver.

"Tim?" She lowered the gun. "Oh, you scared me!"

"Yeah, I know. I didn't think."

"What are you doing here?" She put the gun away and walked closer, still trying to see him in the shadow.

"I might ask you the same thing."

"You can see what I was doing, but *you* here! Do you—"

"Oh, I don't stay here all the time. I saw you coming, only I didn't know who it was." He climbed up and met her. He reached and took hold of her hand. It was warm. She had taken her mitten off to grab the gun. "Where?"

"Your place, of course."

It occurred to Tim that maybe something had happened to old Swiftwater. The old man might have let something slip and let Brunner know who it was that had furnished the tip on the High Chilkao. Brunner was capable of tearing old Swiftwater apart with his hands.

He studied her face. No, he thought, it was nothing like that. She had something on her mind, but she wasn't scared.

He asked, "What's wrong?"

"You couldn't guess!"

"No."

Damn a woman, he thought, why doesn't she say what's on her mind? And he also thought how pretty she was.

"They know all about it, Tim."

"About what?"

"Oh, you can talk to me! About the train."

He moved suddenly as if a knife point had touched him. He doubled his fists; he turned away to keep her from hearing him curse through his teeth. He laughed bitterly. "Well, I'll be damned. He does have his men planted, doesn't he?"

She watched him. Her eyes in the night seemed very dark, a midnight blue, and only the smooth oval of her face was really visible.

"Who is it?" he asked.

"I don't know. Probably I wouldn't tell you anyway, but I *don't* know, and that makes it easy."

"Yeah. One of those Swedes. Why'd you decide to tell me? You shouldn't be taking chances like this for me. You and your dad."

"Dad?"

Evidently she didn't know what Swiftwater had told him about the High Chilkao.

He passed it off by saying, "Well, he's always been pretty decent."

"I didn't want you to get killed."

"Nice fellow!" He meant Brunner, and she knew it.

"I don't know, or even *think* he's going to get rough like that. He might. You know how those things end up." She said with defensive anger, "I'm not calling Croft a murderer, or anything like that. Maybe it's for his sake I came here, so he wouldn't have a killing to blame himself for."

He laughed about it, and the easy sound of his voice took the anger out of her.

She said, "One of you is as bad as the other. You both think you're in the right, that's the main trouble."

"You're engaged to marry Brunner, aren't you?"

He knew she was; he was torturing himself to make her say it.

"Yes."

"Yet here you are coming to warn me, maybe make him lose the biggest prize he ever went out for. Excepting yourself, of course."

"I thought of that. I thought of it all evening. But I didn't want to marry a killer."

He nodded, thinking about Clay, thinking that maybe she *was* marrying a killer.

She said, "I do love him. I care a great deal for him."

"I don't believe you."

Defiantly she asked, "Why not?"

"If you loved that curly wolf you'd never have found it necessary to say that."

"Oh, bosh! Have you been taking a correspondence course in psychology?"

"Correspondence courses are Brunner's line, not mine. I never learned anything unless they beat it into me with an ax handle. Fellows like Ole, they teach me."

"Maybe I shouldn't have come."

"Lynne, wait."

"Let me go."

"Maybe you shouldn't have come, I don't know. But now you're here, I'm going to tell you something." He had not even known he was going to say this, but now he drove straight on, the words coming apparently without his control. "You know when we were kids going to school at Prince Albert? I used to spend half my days thinking about you. I couldn't learn anything in class; they almost booted me out. All I could do was think about you. No, listen, I'm going to finish this. Yes, I thought of you all the time, and still I didn't have the nerve to speak to you when I met you in the hall. Then I went away, and after a while I managed to get over you. Or I thought I did. I knocked around a lot, I went to college and I played a little hockey. I went out with a lot of girls, and then all of a sudden I'd see somebody on the street that made me think of you, and there it'd be all over again. The old pain. Call it pain, that's what it was. Then I woke up in that bunk at Talka, and looked up, and there you were. I couldn't believe it. Then I did believe it, and it was worse than ever. I tell you, when I found out about you and Croft Brunner— Well, forget that. You wouldn't understand. Maybe that's the real reason I'm fighting him. I never analyzed it and I'm not going to try to analyze it now."

She was not pulling back, she simply stared at him with shocked, wide-open eyes.

"You see what a chance you took."

"Tim!" She was really frightened now.

"O.K.," he said, and let her go. "But I still don't believe you're in love with Brunner."

"What *do* you think—that he took me over along with dad's sawmill?"

"Lynne, that's a pretty rough way of saying it."

"Well, he didn't."

"You don't love Brunner. Deep inside you know what he is. A young, rawboned lad that beat my father half to death, a man twice his age. Robbed him and beat him, and you know it."

"Keep still."

"Then Clay. I don't know who got Clay. Maybe it was Ax-Handle Ole, or one of the others. One of the trusted employees of Chipman who slipped down there today—"

"Tim!"

"O.K. I guess I lost my head. What I started out to say in a real nice voice was that you might be scared to see him in a fight and see him for the kind of a man he is."

"Good-by!"

"I'll go along."

"You don't need to."

"I hate to see you go back alone."

He walked beside her. For almost half a mile nothing was said. After that distance he had time to review the things he'd said and feel slightly foolish.

"Angry?" he asked.

She shook her head. "You should have said something. I mean, back in Prince Albert."

He felt a little tingle of hope. "What do you mean?"

"Oh, forget it. That was a long time ago, Tim."

He walked with her until he knew they were just around the long bend from the barricade.

Chapter Nine

HE WATCHED for several minutes after she had disappeared into the night. It was snowing lightly, just enough to put a haze over the moon and obliterate all except the largest stars. The temperature was several degrees below freezing, but walking had made him warm, and he stood with his mackinaw open. He stood there until he had cooled off and had to button his mackinaw again. By that time he had made up his mind.

There was an outside chance that someone was watching him. He walked back toward Chipman for a hundred yards, then he climbed the bank and hunted his way through the forest, as he had done once before, until the lights of Talka lay below.

His first idea had been to get hold of an engine and a couple of cars and crash the barricade, but he needed men to follow him and tear up the track.

He sat on a log and appraised the state of things.

The mill was going on a skeleton night shift, the interior brightly lighted. Post lights burned here and there across the big yards, leaving wide areas of shadow between. An engine with a single car attached stood outside the shed, letting out a soft hiss of steam. There was no movement around her. She had steam, but he hated to guess how much. Probably not enough to get up the grade to the main track, and besides, there would be switching to do.

One engine here, that meant two others down at Vermilion. One of those would likely be in the shop, the other would be starting back before dawn with a string of empties. That one would have pressure up. That was the one he wanted.

However, he had to get hold of Lars Halseth and his strong Swedes, and the phone wire had been cut off.

He was familiar with Talka from the old days, and though a lot of things had been changed, the old crankup telephones were the same as ever, and there was the same little bobtailed switchboard up at the railroad shack.

He walked beside the tracks, not too close beside them, keeping in shadow. The shack was dingy and dark. It

had been years since the windows were washed. There
was no smoke from the chimney. It opened with a loud
complaint, and he stepped inside.

"Hello!" he said, just in case, but nobody answered
him.

He groped, found the old corset-shaped stove, the
switchboard. It was impossible to work without a light.
He had to chance it. He struck a match.

The wires were plugged in crisscross on the switchboard in a manner he did not understand. As the match
burned down it occurred to him that the wires to Chipman might have been torn down outside, but this he
doubted, because it would have been illegal, and Brunner was careful to stay inside the letter of the law.

He lit another match. This time he lit the lamp. In
an old bunk against the far wall lay some dusty gray
blankets. He hung one over each of the windows. Then
he went back to the switchboard. There were a couple of
spare plugs, but he had no idea where to insert them.

Then he heard a footstep, the creak of a board, and
the door opened.

He stood up, for some reason expecting it to be Brunner himself, but it was a young fellow he'd never seen
before.

"Hello."

"Oh, hello," said Tim, and he could see that the fellow
was not suspicious of him, only curious. "I'm the ac-
countant." It was the first thing that came into his head.

"Oh." He was looking at the blankets over the windows.

"They told me I'd better do that or I'd have Ax-
Handle Ole snooping around."

"Sure, that dumb bastard. He snoops everywhere."

"You know anything about this?" he asked, nodding
toward the switchboard.

"Sure. What do you want to do, talk to Vermilion?"
He stared at Tim. "Well, I don't know."

"It's pretty important. I have to talk to those fellows
and I can't go up there. I'm not going to get shot trying
to talk to them about that legal business down in Victoria."

"Oh!" the fellow said, as if he understood all about it.
"Well, all I was thinking, the line might be down. The
porcupines are always working on those poles, tearing

the wires off. Last week they had 'em on the ground out near Squaw Gulch."

He plugged the wires in where Tim had been intending to, went to a wall phone, and cranked very hard. He kept cranking and cranking. "Nope."

"Sit down and have a smoke. We'll probably have to wake 'em up."

Tim took the man's place and cranked steadily for more than a minute. Steve would be in his place asleep. He'd have to be lucky to wake him. But that fellow on watch would hear the bell. A bell would be pretty unusual at Chipman, and there was a chance he would investigate.

"Guess you'll have to try tomorrow."

Tim kept working the crank. When his right arm grew tired he used his left.

"Hallo!" a voice shouted through the receiver into his ear. It was Steve.

"Hello. I'm down at Talka."

"Who is this?"

He couldn't tell him with the fellow listening. "I'm at Talka."

"You said that. So what?"

"Who is this?"

"Riika."

"Where's the other fellow?"

"Who, Tim?"

That's what he wanted. "That's who I am."

"Tim? What the hell? Are you drunk?"

"No. I'm calling about that business—that unfinished business, you know. Can you get hold of Mr. Halseth?"

"What the hell you talkin' about?" Steve was shouting. "Mr. Halseth! You mean Lars? Damn it, why don't you say Lars? What's the matter with you?"

Couldn't he guess there might be someone listening? Tim longed to get the big Finlander by the throat. At that moment he seemed dumber than all the oxen in the universe.

Tim said with careful significance, "Wait a minute. Here's the phone operator. Mr. Brunner's own private employee. He's right here. Maybe I should have him talk to you."

"Oh!" said Steve, collapsing as he got it through his head. "You down there? He don't know who you are?

You get an ax handle behind your ear. You take one hell of a chance. You—"

"Sure. Well, you get word to Mr. Halseth, will you? Tell him it was necessary for us to alter our plans. The agreement still holds, but an emergency has arisen. We will have to conclude the deal tonight."

"Yah."

"Tell him to be there with his witnesses at the appointed hour. Tell them to have their pen and ink handy."

"Yah, ax handles!"

"A little before sunup."

"O.K., Tim. Don't you worry your head, Tim."

He hung up. He unplugged the wires. The fellow was watching him, smoking, and smoking too fast. He was burning his cigarette down as fast as he could drag the smoke in. The ash got long, and when he went to knock it on the floor, a tremble of his hand shook it instead on his shirt front.

Then Tim noticed a headset on the board and knew that Steve's answer had been audible to him.

"Well, I guess I'll go down and hit the hay," the fellow said, making an effort to seem casual.

"No."

He looked scared. "What?"

"No, kid. You're not much of an actor. We better stick together."

He wanted to run, but there was no place to go except through the door, and Tim was blocking it.

"You do what I say, just what I say, and you won't get hurt. No broken neck, nothing."

"O.K. I won't cause any trouble."

Tim watched his eyes. He was scared enough, but just to make sure, he felt inside his mackinaw the way men do when they loosen a pistol in an armpit holster. He wished he *did* have a pistol in an armpit holster, but maybe it was just as well. He grinned at him, and the fellow looked as though he were stricken by ptomaine.

"Blow out the light."

He did. He came straight to the door. They went outside together. Tim looked around. No Ax-Handle Ole. No anybody. Still the fine snow drifted down through the night, the moon and stars hazy and magnified.

"Handcar."

"Sure."

The fellow knew right where it was. They carried it out of the shed and set it on the rails. It took scarcely a pound of pressure on its pumping mechanism to start it down the grade.

It was long past midnight, but there was still not the slightest hint of dawn when they sighted Vermilion. The phone line leading to Talka was strung along the trunks of jack-spruce trees paralleling the tracks. He stopped and told his companion to break the wire. He decided that breaking it wasn't enough, and told him to take down about a hundred feet of it and coil it up and bring it to the handcar. When he did, Tim stepped out and hurled it as far as he could toward the river.

"You didn't need to make it that tough on me," the fellow said.

"You get paid by the day, don't you?"

He didn't say anything.

Night lights burned in the railroad office and in a couple of buildings on the lake front. One of the repair-shop doors was open, a square of dim, ruddy light. Men talked, their voices coming across the distance, their actual words undistinguishable. The engine and a string of cars were pulled out and ready. A man walked along swinging an electric hand lantern. The voices had stopped now, and he could hear the thin, rackety sound of a radio tuned to some all-night record program down in the States.

They let the handcar coast down to the railroad yards. The switch was open, carrying them to the same siding as the train.

"Stop it," said Tim.

"What are you going to do?" He was getting scared again. "There's no use dragging me into this. If you—"

"You do as I say and not the slightest harm will come to you."

"I'll have to get out of the country if Brunner ever—"

"Come up to my place, then. Maybe I'll give you a job. Anybody can work for me if he's willing to take his wages on credit."

They were now quite close to the engine—close enough to smell it, the combination of burning pitch pine and lubricants.

The door to a tool house stood open. "In there!" said

Tim, and before the fellow realized what was up, he had closed the door and latched it.

"Listen, kid," Tim said through the crack of the door, "you raise any hell, or break out of there while I'm around, and I'll open you up so the wind can blow through. The repair crew will find you when they come on shift at eight."

He walked on. The engineer was leaning from the cab of the little engine, talking to someone on the ground. "Well, as I said to the missus—" the engineer was saying, but that was all Tim caught. He walked straight on, casually, so as not to attract notice, thinking it would be a hell of a lot harder to run a bluff on that engine crew than it had been on that punk he'd just locked in the shed.

He needed a gun. He wondered if there was anyone over in town he could borrow one from. It was more than a mile, and that would take too long.

When he was alive, old Harry Sanford used to keep a rifle back of his desk at the office. He went there and let himself in. No one was around. He pawed around in some dusty junk near the table, and there was the gun, a lever-action Winchester, caliber 405. "Four hundred and five!" he laughed. "What an old smokehouse!" He could blast the whole train off the track with that.

It was loaded. He carried it outside and walked down beside the train, on the opposite side from where the engineer and his friend were talking. He found the shadow of a snow fence and waited, nervous now, very tense, clutching the rifle too hard.

After what seemed at least half an hour, the fireman climbed to the cab, opened the firebox, and commenced stuffing wood in. The engineer stopped talking. He tooted the whistle twice, looked up and down the track to see if anyone was coming, and pushed the throttle.

Forcing himself to walk, Tim Chipman left the snow fence, climbed to one of the flatcars, and lay down flat on his stomach.

No one saw him. With a great noise of expanding steam the engine gained speed. A switch rattled under the wheels. They were past the tool house. Its door was still bolted, its window in place. There was no sound from its prisoner. With the train gone, he would probably have guts enough to break out, but it would take

him a couple of hours to get up the track and patch
the phone line, and two hours would be all Tim needed
—if everything went right.

The train carried no crew except the engineer and
fireman. It pulled seven flatcars. The little narrow-
gauge line owned no more than fifteen or sixteen. He
could lay claim to no more than five. He had plenty of
time to think. He measured the length of the car he
was on, and planned how those big logs of the High
Chilkao could be carried. Sawed in five segments, some
of those big sticks would just make a trainload.

He rode for a long time. Dawn was coming, but slowly,
through fog. The fog prevented him from seeing any
distance, but certain landmarks along the cuts told him
that Talka was just ahead.

He walked forward then, climbed over the tender, and
stood looking down inside the engine cab.

Neither man saw him. Their backs were toward him
as they watched the track ahead. The little engine
clanked along slowly. The headlamp was still on, re-
flecting back white against the billow of fog. Here and
there the fog opened, but it was settling from the high
country, and they were climbing, and each new cloud
was more dense than the one they had just left.

The fireman said something about the steam. The
engineer glanced at it. Tim was crouched with the rifle
only a few feet above. The engineer seemed to be almost
looking at him, but he turned away and said, "Put in
your big stuff. I don't think we'll be pulling out very
early today."

"I got a gun on you," Tim said quietly, and the sound
of his voice made them almost jump out of the cab.

"You damned fool!" cried the fireman, with fright
putting a crazy edge on his voice. "Quit pointing that
gun."

Tim shortened the barrel, the stock under his right
arm. "Just take it easy," he said, making his voice
steady, "and nobody will get hurt."

"You're Tim Chipman!" said the engineer, peering at
him from under the pulled-down bill of his cap. "Tim,
what the hell! You know me, Charley Makin."

"My engine, Charley."

"Huh?"

"Yeah. I own a third of this line. That's legal. That

entitles me to one engine and five or six cars. I'm taking
'em. Now—"

"You can't."

"Well, I thought you'd act like that, so that's why
the gun."

It made it tougher, the man's knowing him. It made
it more likely he'd try to ignore the gun, and if he did,
Tim didn't know what his own action would be. One
thing he vowed not to do was pull the trigger.

The engineer thought it over for a while, standing
crouched a little, his hands opening and closing. Then
he blew out his breath and sat down again.

"I got no argument with you, or with that old moose
gun, either. I just put in my eight hours and draw my
pay. I just do my job."

They were moving through a dense layer of fog now,
a fog that reflected the light of the headlamp in a white
flare, and the steep cutaway bank at their left was seen
as through a layer of milk.

"Ease off," said Tim.

The engineer did. The train quickly slowed against
the grade.

"Turn off the headlamp."

It left the cab quite dark, but he was able to see,
partly from the foggy dawn, partly from the cracks of
the firebox.

"There's a switch. I know where it is. Don't try to go
through it."

The engineer nodded grimly.

"Turn the switch, then come back in the engine," he
said to the fireman. And when he moved in response,
"Not now. Wait till the train stops." He had calmed
himself. He even managed to laugh. "The way us Chipmans run our end of the railroad, nobody gets off until
she stops."

Neither of the others thought it was very funny. The
sides of the cut fell away. There was little fog in the
valley and the gray shapes of the mill buildings were
visible. A tractor and trailer with a load consisting of
big log segments were just coming in with the headlamps on.

The engineer stopped.

"Now!" Tim said to the fireman.

He got down, almost fell on the unexpected pitch of

the ground, and ran forward to the switch. He turned it, the simple process of lifting a weighted bar up and over. Some snow and forest detritus had accumulated in the unused track opening, but it closed well enough, and the engine moved over it.

Reluctantly the fireman climbed back to the moving cab.

The engineer said, "Barricade up above. What in hell are we supposed to do there?"

"Blow your whistle."

"Hah!" he said with a sour laugh. Then it occurred to him that Tim had some help waiting. "O' course. You got your boys there."

Tim was not sure. It would take some doing to rouse Halseth and his Swedes and move them there in time. Besides, the details had never been worked out. They'd have brains enough to know they had to tear down the barricade. Well, if the worst came about, maybe they could buck their way through with this engine. The front end of it was specially made to scoop logs off the track.

Below, in the mill yard, the truck with its timber was moving at a bare crawl. The electric lights, still on, looked pale. A man was walking down from the main office. He did not recognize him. It wasn't Brunner. Suddenly the man's notice was attracted to the train— the strange sight of a train not turning at the switch, but following the rusty road toward Chipman. There he stood, watching, as long as Tim could see him.

They passed the little station shack. He noticed, dark against the gray-streaked windows, the blankets he had hung up the night before. He wondered how the fellow was doing in the tool house back at Vermilion. Quite obviously he had still not repaired the telephone line, or there would have been more of a reception here.

Less than a half mile now would bring him to the barricade. He watched the country appearing and reappearing as they passed in and out of cuts. Everything looked different in the fog.

He decided to blow the whistle. He had arranged for no exact signal, so he blew it in a series of short blasts, eight or ten of them.

"How far is it?" he called to the engineer.

"I don't know. I never been up here."

"Slow down." He reached for the throttle. Hell, thought Chipman, we're barely away from Talka camp. "Wait."

They kept booming along. Here and there snow and rubble had blown over the track, causing the engine to weave and hesitate, and then seem to go on harder than ever.

Over the rattle of machinery he seemed to hear a distant shout. He wanted to lean from the engine and listen, but that would have placed him too close to the fireman, who might have it in his mind to go for the gun.

He moved backward, climbing with the aid of his left hand and right elbow, getting back to the fuel car.

A gun cracked. No bullet, though. It seemed close, but when he got his wits about him he realized it had been as much as two hundred yards off.

The engineer was reaching for the throttle.

"No!" Tim shouted.

Either Riika had torn the barricade down or he hadn't. Either way, there was no stopping. If the barricade was down, the engine would roll through; if it was still up . . . Well, he tried not to think of that.

They emerged from timber and clanked along the unrepaired rails. Successive layers of fog whipped around them. Men were firing from down the track, warning them to stop. And yes, the damned barricade was still up.

He cursed himself for making Lars leave the rifles behind. What chance did those Swedes have with their ax handles while every Brunner man had a gun under his arm? But the truth was that he'd expected maybe one man on the barricade, and he asleep.

He lay face down on the tender. He caught a brief glimpse of the engineer and fireman leaping from the cab. A man was in the middle of the track, waving a rifle over his head. Then he was running, clambering through trees up the hillside. Tim spraddled his legs, dug in the toes of his boots, grabbed the metal of the tender; he even closed his eyes. Then they hit it, but not with the crash he expected. The sound was a dull roar, a booming like drums, and shock almost propelled him head foremost into the engine cab.

He clung. He managed to get to the cab feet first.

The engine was still upright. It was moving along; it made a bump-bump sound. It was derailed, he thought, rolling along on the ties.

He leaned out to look. The wheel flanges still hung to the rails. That bumping came from a log wedged and dragging.

He could not resist a whoop of elation. He turned and shouted back through cupped hands, "Ax-Handle Ole, you dim-wit! Ole, what the hell? Come on and fight!"

"Tim, Tim!" he heard Steve Riika call somewhere in the twilight void of timber and fog.

Tim knew enough about engines to get the thing stopped. Men were all around him, his men, fifteen or twenty of them, some with ax handles, some with rifles.

"Cut off those last two cars."

"Hey?"

"Don't ask, just cut 'em loose. I'll take no more than I got coming."

The flatcars coasted slowly back and were hidden by fog.

"Who was doing that shooting?" he asked.

"Not us," one of the gun-carrying men said, "but maybe it's about time."

"Not unless we have to."

"We'll have to." He was looking down the track, expecting them to come.

"No, there's only three or four of 'em. They'll want it two to one on their side. They'll have to get reinforcements from Talka. In the meantime we'll start tearing up track."

Chapter Ten

No one had thought to bring tools, but there were a few in a box on the tender. With these they fell to work tearing up track. Dawn came and the fog lifted. Slowly the train moved toward its new home in Chipman, pulling its track in behind it.

Johnson came up from the Talka boundary with word that Brunner and a group of men had arrived.

"All right," Tim said, taking the rifle. "I'll go down and see what he wants."

"You couldn't guess?" asked Johnson, grinning.

His men were going to follow him, but he told them to stay back. Some of them followed anyway, but fifty or sixty paces in the rear. He stopped with a view of the barricade, where about twenty men were gathered. One of the men was Ax-Handle Ole; another was Brunner.

Tim stopped, and Brunner, seeing him, called, "Come along, you'll be safe enough. What do you want to see me about?"

"I can say it from here. I took no more than my legal right." Give or take a couple of flatcars, he was thinking. "Now I'm warning you. You and your gang stay on your side of the line."

The words infuriated Brunner. "Threaten me, will you?"

Brunner had not spoken loudly. He had rather spoken through clenched teeth, with muscles set at the sides of his jaw, but the force behind it clearly carried his words across the distance.

Brunner started forward. He carried a rifle. His head was lowered; his eyes were fixed on Tim. He had a stiff-legged, stud-horse manner of walking that always served as a barometer of his fury.

"Leave your gun behind!" Tim cried.

"You think I need it?"

He tossed it aside, and Tim tossed his gun aside. Brunner walked straight on. Tim planted himself, digging his hobs in the ties. It took a minute or so for Brunner to travel the distance. Then, when it seemed they were ready to collide, he came to a halt.

They were about three steps apart. Brunner looked the taller, thinner man up and down.

"I'm here. What the hell are you going to do about it?" When Tim made no immediate answer, he jerked his head toward the bend with its torn-up track. "You think you can get away with that?"

"The train? It's part of my third of the line."

"You don't own one spoke or one rail. Under the laws of the province you've just committed armed assault and robbery."

"Then turn it over to the authorities."

"Maybe I'll do that."

"Then you're wasting your time here."

"I could take you into court and beat you out of your teeth. But it'd take time. I don't want to take time licking a Chipman."

It would also drag the whole railroad business into the open, and force Brunner to keep the line open from Chipman mill to Vermilion all the time that the legal actions dragged along. That's what Brunner meant when he said he didn't want to take time to lick a Chipman.

And now the track was up, and there was no way he could force the cars and engine back. His impotence made him furious. He called Tim Chipman a vile name, lunged forward, and swung.

Tim seemed to give ground. Instead, at the final instant, he stepped inside. He took Brunner's blow short of its aim. He hooked a left and sent an upper cut with the right to the base of Brunner's ribs.

Brunner's anger had carried him too far. The upper cut momentarily robbed him of strength, but it gave him back his fighter's brains. Although anger told him to charge on and carry his man before him, his craftiness made him clinch and retreat.

He took lefts and rights with bent arms in front of him. He saw when Tim let the distance between them lengthen and start a right for his head. To give himself another second or two, he went down.

A whoop went up from the Chipman crowd, for to them it seemed that Brunner had been poleaxed by that looping right. It hadn't touched him, though. It had passed inches above his head and instead had the effect of carrying Tim off balance.

Brunner was himself again. He charged from a crouch. He carried his taller, less stockily built opponent before him. They tripped and fell. As they went down, Brunner doubled his right knee and sank it in Chipman's groin.

Tim Chipman was blind and sick from pain. Instinct told him to hold tight, but there was no one to hold to. He tried to get to his feet. He was down again as Brunner sprang him and gave him the hobs.

By that time Lars was coming and Steve Riika was coming. Others were behind them. Tim Chipman was doubled over, arms wrapped around his head, and Brunner, grunting each time, was booting him.

Riika hurled a slab of rock that caught Brunner a glancing blow across the back. He was still intent on kicking Tim's head in, but the melee caught him and carried him with it. There were ax handles, rocks, and fists. Men were down and given the hobs. Over it all rose the bellow of Ax-Handle Ole, who, swinging his ax handle, charged an opening through all the Chipman men and then charged back again.

He saw a Chipman man on the ground. He stopped in order to trample him. It was a mistake, for there was another Chipman man behind him. He went down, clubbed by a railroad spike. He had dropped his ax handle. It was behind him. He did not know that. One of Lars Halseth's Swedes made for him with a shovel from the engine box. Ole, unarmed, retreated and took the blow with an upflung hand. He saw a club of pine at some distance and ran for it. The sight of him, apparently galloping in retreat, arms covering the back of his head, took the heart out of his men, and they followed him, forming a rough phalanx for their protection. The Chipman forces were content to see them go.

Men were down, two from each crowd. One of them lay limp as death, a trickle of blood running from an ear, from the side of his mouth. They turned him over. He was a log bucker named Peterson, one of the Chipman crew.

On the instant everyone was watching for some sign of life.

"Damn you," Brunner said to Ole and the others. "Why didn't you stay back like I told you? What if he's dead?"

One of them cried, "Self-defense. He was swinging an ax handle."

"Self-defense on his own ground? How the hell would you like to go into court with that?"

He turned and watched as Steve Riika examined Peterson. Then life came into the fallen man's muscles and he had strength enough to moan and curse and spit a mouthful of blood. Brunner grunted and turned to look at Tim, and that sight was more to his liking.

Tim was on his feet, but he needed a tree for support. The blow to his groin had left him sick. He tried to vomit but there was nothing in his stomach. His face was cut and bleeding from the hobs. His mackinaw was open, his shirt was torn, his chest and stomach were bare, and blood from his face and neck had run down, smearing him.

"Tim, how you feel?" asked Brunner. When his voice didn't get through, he asked it again: "Hey, Tim, how you feel?"

Brunner waited until Tim found him with his eyes. Then he said, "Tim, there's a sample. And don't forget who started it. You! You, Tim. You!"

Chapter Eleven

Tim Chipman stood over the washbasin and looked at his face in a rusty oblong of mirror. It was swollen, his eyes were puffed almost shut, his face looked strangely round. One of his cheeks was all purple. He had been cut up some by Brunner's hobnails, but the heavy boot toes had really done the business.

"Twice, now!" he said. "One of these times maybe I'll learn my lesson."

Behind him, Steve named Brunner a suitable name. "That's dirty fighting, kick a man there. Even barroom fighting, that's dirty. Dirty even for lumberjack."

"Nothing's dirty for a lumberjack. When it's a lumberjack, the rules don't count."

He supervised tearing up the track, and when that was well along he did some surveying on the other end. He needed more men, and he needed a bulldozer. There was a bulldozer at his Belle Creek camp, but it needed new bearings. He put some horse scrapers to work. To get additional men he closed down all his operations except the one on Nokewin Lake. On Chilkao he started building a winter camp. Through those days he scarcely found time to sleep, certainly no time to worry about his battered face, or about Brunner.

Then payday was coming up.

He went down Mad River by canoe to the lake and followed the edge of it to the Beaver Mill, where D.W. Garson was president and general manager. Garson was gone, either to Vancouver or down to the States. His son had been left in charge. That personable young man was certain that his father would be interested in securing a quantity of white pine saw logs the following spring and Chipman could depend on the Beaver Mill's meeting anyone else's price. Tim told him that he needed a substantial cash advance, but unfortunately young Garson lacked authority to make it. He wanted logs. He begged Tim to wait a few days. When Tim said no he tried to telephone his father, and finally got through to the hotel in Vancouver, but Garson had checked out.

It was midnight then. Tim spent the night there and

continued on by canoe to the Macardle Mill, a run-down nest of red-painted buildings at the foot of Beaver Lake, on a rail line that traversed some little hills to Prince Albert.

Macardle himself was on hand, a huge, deaf old man, roughly clad and smelling of pitch. Like most sawmill men, Macardle had been reduced to cutting the cheaper varieties of wood, and even with times good he frequently had trouble marketing the finished product. White pine, however, would be a different matter, and he chuckled at the idea of having the lumber buyers stand drinks for a change.

The matter of advance payment took some of the pleasure out of it for the Scot, however, and when Tim talked in exact amounts he kept shouting, "What? What?" fooling around with the control on his hearing aid. There had been talk going around about the High Chilkao, and Chipman was an old concern, so at last he put his pen to a checkbook, and Tim was in good shape for another month.

Tim left his canoe and took Macardle's teakettle logging engine to Prince Albert, where he converted the check into cash. At Prince Albert he hired a motor launch around the other way to Nokewin Lake, where he paid off on the dot, but he was a day late at Chipman.

"We been having trouble," Steve Riika told him. "Dick Poole's outfit?"

The big Finlander looked surprised. "Yah. You already know, Tim?"

"I'm a good guesser. I'm one hell of a good guesser."

He followed Tim, saying, "Now, I wouldn't start any trouble with Dick. He's one hell of a fine logger."

He turned and said, "Only four men knew I was going to grab that engine the other day. I was one and you were one. Lars was one and Dick was one."

He hunted out Dick Poole. "Dick," he said, "I hear your crew is dissatisfied. I hear some of 'em are going to quit."

Dick got up, broad and truculent and apprehensive. "You were late with their pay. They don't like a tin-bucket spread, either. Nose-bag show, that's what they call it. Some of 'em heard there were jobs down at Talka. You can't blame me for that."

Eight or ten men were standing around, listening. They were in the bunkhouse, but the door was open, and the voices carried. More men kept coming, some of them through the door, most of them to stop outside.

"That scab camp of Brunner's! Well, let's settle it now. You want to bellyache, bellyache to me. Get it over with. If you don't like it here, pack up your gear and go."

Nobody said anything. Poole sat on the bench, opening and closing his hands, staring at the boards. Finally a little fellow named Palaski said, "He said you couldn't meet the payroll. He said you gone broke. If you go broke, who pay us off? We can't work all winter for nothing."

"Who told you that?"

Palaski knew he shouldn't have said it. He stood looking at Poole.

"Well, Dick," Tim said to him.

Dick Poole leaped to his feet. "All right, I didn't want to see the boys spend a winter on the cuff. I still don't. Let's do what he says. Let's pack up and get to hell out of here. There's a job waiting for every able-bodied man of you down at Talka."

After some hesitation, one man started packing his war bag. Another followed him. Just two—that was all.

Angry frustration showed in Poole's face. Tim knew that half of them must have seemed receptive at some previous time. Poole stood looking from one man to the next.

"How about you, Nels?" he called to a Norwegian.

"No. I ain't working for no scab camp."

"Why, you said—"

"I don't care what I said."

"Get out," Tim said.

"I'll get out in my own good time!" Poole shouted, and took a step forward. Both of his fists were doubled as though ready to swing, but Tim's response surprised him.

Tim feinted a left and came up with a right that smashed him to the floor.

Poole got to his hands and knees and remained that way for half a minute with his head down and blood running from his mouth. At last he was able to lift his head and bring his eyes into focus.

"I'll get you for that, Chipman!" he whispered hoarsely.

"Get me now while I'm handy."

Poole crawled backward, got hold of the edge of a bench, and got to his feet. He groped and found his bunk. Blood kept running over his chin and he kept wiping it away with the palms of his hands, smearing it into a red mask. He gathered his stuff in his arms, blankets, clothes, a gun and holster, a couple of books, a portable radio. Somehow he managed to carry it all.

"You dirty fink!" somebody shouted, and hurled a boot at him as he got to the door.

The boot struck the casing and bounded back inside. He did not look around. He made no move to use the gun. Without saying anything the two men followed him.

Tim turned, looking all around, and said, "Thanks."

A rawboned young man with bristly red hair elbowed his way to the fore and said, "Chipman!"

"Yes?"

"Give it to me straight. You really think you can pay off this big handle when spring comes?"

"I'll pay every cent. Maybe I'll have to sell my timber holdings, but I'll pay."

"That's good enough for me."

The departure of Dick Poole was like a fifty-pound load taken off Tim Chipman's shoulders. He felt fine, he felt fine all over. He noticed that his knuckles were skinned. He didn't mind that, either.

He met Steve Riika. "What the hell?" said Steve, looking at his hands.

"You should see Dick's jaw. He was the lad, Steve, and now he's gone and his friends with him. The rest of the boys are for me. We'll take out timber now. We'll timber like hell."

Work boomed along. One man quit and another was taken out to Chinook Inlet for a gall-bladder operation, but they picked up a few men from outside and remained about even. The rail line was at Chilkao, and rapidly on its way to Mad River Canyon. Sidings at the home camp were pulled for extra rails. Snow came and the work went on. The snow melted and came again and melted again. Then for a time it was as warm as spring—"old wife's summer," as the Cousin Jacks called it. The first great trees of the Chilkao came crashing to earth and were bucked and yarded ready for the first trip on the rail line. He had contracted for winter grub at a wholesaler's at Chinook Inlet, but there was insufficient snow to haul it in by sled trailer as the warm weather held.

The line to Mad River had been completed forty-eight hours when the big blizzard, so long anticipated, at last howled down from the north. It lasted for five days, intermittently clearing and coming on again. It was warm for most of that time as the snow deepened. Then it cleared, the wind died, and there descended a sharp cold. It was zero, and the next day it was five below, and then ten, and it was apparent now that the long winter had set in.

A routine established itself. The timber was cut and skidded by a system evolved to fit the circumstances. Although they were short on machinery, there was one major factor to their advantage, and that was the steady grade of the ridge side, the absence of gullies, the smoothness of the earth and lack of undergrowth that made the Chilkao ground easy to timber. Lacking trucks, several old-time donkey engines were put into service, and logs were skidded along chutes glazed by means of hot water that turned to ice. Once over the Knob the grade was in their favor. That made rail-roading easy. The loaded cars had a steady downgrade all the way to Mad River; then, when they were light and empty, the engine pulled them back. For two days, when the engine was laid up for a welding job, they got along quite well by coasting under load, and then returning a car at a time, empty, pulled by a four-horse team.

Logs, once they were delivered to the canyon edge on Mad River, were not immediately dropped over the steep side. Temporarily they were yarded by means of a small skidder; later, after the river ice thickened, they would be lowered by means of high tackle, thus eliminating the splinter and tangle that might lead to a disastrous log jam when the Mad went out in the spring.

The supplies arrived from Chinook. It made everyone feel better to be off a diet of beans, pancakes, and rice pudding. Things went smoothly; almost too smoothly, Riika said. Not a whisper had been heard from the

Talka side. Brunner was gone, they heard. Tim was apprehensive of legal action because of the railroad. There was none.

Now it was the second week of December. Tim Chipman had gone from the home camp to the Knob and down to Mad River all since getting up three hours before daylight that morning. McCabe had knocked the tops from two very large Douglas spruce trees, one on each side of the canyon, and they had been fitted with guy cables. Today they were trying to string a cable across the canyon, and were having their troubles. Something was wrong with the bull block, a friction aggravated by the twenty-below cold. For the second time Chipman was aloft. The block seemed to be freed, and someone was calling him from below. He went down and stood over a campfire trying to thaw his hands out, listening while Buster Dibble, the cook's helper from Chipman, tried to say something.

"Fire away, Buzz," Tim said, laughing at the kid's excitement. "What's wrong? Has Brunner burned us out?"

"A mountie's come for you."

"Just one?"

"Yeah."

"He didn't come *for* me. Not a mountie. I know those lads. If he came to take me away, I wouldn't find it out from you. I'd find it out from him."

They decided to take a short cut. That required snowshoes. Winter darkness settled early. There was a long misty twilight, followed by a gray evening. A few stars came out. Tim had to go slowly because Buster was unused to snowshoes and the spraddle-legged walk their use demanded. Finally, well past suppertime, they crested the last hill, and the home camp, with its frosted, lighted windows, lay below them.

He went straight to the main office. It was lighted, and smoke came from the chimney. He tried the door. It was stuck in ice. He shouldered it open. As he expected, there was the mounted policeman, waiting for him.

"Hello, Constable," he said, recognizing his rank.

The mountie had been sitting with his boots propped toward the stove, passing the time with a paper-back novel that he had found in the room. He laid it aside, apparently trying to remember just where he had found it. Then he waited a few seconds for the rush of white vapor to clear away and for Tim to walk into the lamplight.

"You're Chipman."

"Yes."

"Constable Nevens, Fort McCrae."

"Oh, sure." Tim tried to remember if they'd ever met before. He decided they hadn't. Nevens was a young fellow, younger than himself, so there was no chance he'd been on the force before Tim went away.

Nevens waited for him to get his heavy coat off. Then he said, "I understand you ran a rail line from Granite Knob to Mad River Canyon."

"That's right." Anyway, thought Tim, he's not accusing me of stealing the engine and cars.

"Yes. Well, it's been reported that the line was laid across the Lippel home claim."

That was a new one on Tim. He had never heard of a Lippel home claim. He signified that by shrugging and laughing while going to the stove and rubbing his hands.

"You haven't heard of it?"

"No. That's all timber land up there. My dad logged most of it off when I was a little kid. There's young timber on lots of it now, large enough for pulpwood. I never knew of a man to raise so much as a row of radishes up there."

Nevens gave the location. Apparently he had memorized it. Tim walked to the map, smeared over with charcoal from his diagraming, and found the spot.

"Here. Oh, that's the old Randolph cut. Dad bought that from Davey Randolph. That was all white pine, just a little Douglas. What was that name? Lippel?"

Now, as he tried to remember, it seemed that he *could* remember someone by the name of Lippel.

"Yes. Did you lay rails across there?"

Tim nodded.

"Well, I'm sorry if this is going to cause you any trouble, Chipman, but the claimant of that ground has objected to the line. In fact, he's enjoined you from further use of it until your right has been cleared in court."

"We're a hell of a long way from court."

The policeman set his jaw and said, "I'm sorry. There's

no point in losing your temper with me. I'm merely following—"

"Sure, I know. They give you a paper and tell you
this is it. Where did you say you came from? Fort
McCrae?"

"My assignment isn't from there."

"Where, then?"

"Prince Albert."

"Can I look at the papers?"

The policeman got them from a leather folder and
gave them to him. Tim read through them rapidly.

"Yeah. This does it. This blocks the rail line."

"Can't you go around?"

"I could have, before the snow, if I'd had more steel."

The papers had been issued at the request of someone who called himself Frank P. Lippel.

"Do you know this Lippel?"

"He's the owner. Claimant, anyway. He claimed the
land as a farm site twenty-seven years ago."

"Farm site! Stumps and rocks. Moss, pine needles,
and side hills. No one ever lived there. I guess there is
a cabin back in the bush, but a farm site! I asked if you
knew Lippel—before this came up, I mean."

"No."

"How much time do I have before this goes into
effect?"

"I'm afraid none whatever. I'll have to go up there
tomorrow and post it. If I were you, I'd go down to
P.A. and see the magistrate. Perhaps you could con-
vince him of your unnecessary hardship, and—"

"Yeah." He was thinking that this was Brunner's doing,
and Brunner would have made pretty certain about
convincing that magistrate. Besides, he didn't have
time to make the long journey to Prince Albert.

"Where's Lippel?"

"He came with me."

"Here?"

"Oh, no. I left him," he seemed slightly abashed at
saying it, "at the mill down there."

"Talka?"

"Yes."

"Well, he's their boy."

"Understand, I'm taking no sides in this. He merely
asked if he could—"

"Sure, I know. You've just got a job to do. Why'd he say he was coming? To move back on the old claim?"

"So he said."

"Oh, hell!" Tim said, holding his head from laughter.

"Really! He said he intended to live up there while he waits for his wife."

"A pack rat couldn't live in that shack."

"No? Well, that's none of my worry. I'm just telling you what he said."

"Could I take that notice and post it for you, save you the trouble?"

"I'm afraid not. Not that I don't trust you. It's just that I can't do it. You understand."

"Sure," said Tim wearily. "I understand."

At dawn he went upcountry with the constable and watched him locate some old boundary markers along the western side of the claim. There he tacked up a No Trespassing sign and left.

Lars Halseth, who had come around to look at it, plastered the paper with a spurt of snoose and said, "Hah! He tank that stop railroad train?"

Tim said, "Well, wait till he's out of the country."

He went around asking all the old-timers if they remembered Lippel. Finally he found a couple who did. Later that day he found Lippel mentioned in the company correspondence. He had a claim, true enough, but it seemed to have been abandoned, and after that the ownership had apparently fallen to the Chipman Company when the entire area on that side of Chilkoos Lake had been adjudged unfit for agriculture.

But proving that would take time. It would require a journey to Victoria. It would take some slow grinding of the law, and in the meantime he might well go broke with an idle crew and his logs stalled against the mountie's legal barricade.

It was lucky they had not sent the engine through, because the next morning Constable Nevens was back with his man.

Tim was just having breakfast. He stood up, his mouth filled with ham and flapjacks, and looked at the skinny, big-beaked, chinless man who had stopped in the doorway, apparently not knowing whether it was quite safe to follow the constable or not.

"You're Lippel?" Tim asked.

"Yes," he said, gulping his Adam's apple into exaggerated movement.

Nevens said, "Come on in so I can close the door. We don't want to freeze the man out."

It was obvious that Nevens was not too proud of his companion.

Lippel quick-stepped it inside. He shot glances all around. His eyes had a swift, weasel quality. He carried with him the odor of alcohol.

"I understand we're going to be neighbors," said Tim.

"What?"

"I say we're to be neighbors. Or don't you intend to move in up there?"

"Oh, there! Sure."

"You build that cabin?"

"Yes."

"When?"

"I forgot."

"It *was* a while ago. When'd you take up the claim?"

He named the exact date with a readiness that told Tim he had memorized it.

"Well, welcome home. You'll know some of the old-timers, I suppose."

"I don't remember anybody much. It's been quite a while. You timber men never did me any favors. Fact is, you did your best to run me off. Why should I remember anybody?"

Tim tried to estimate his age, comparing it with the date of the claim.

He asked unexpectedly, "When were you born?"

Lippel immediately had his guard up. "I don't think that's any of your business."

In a rough voice, almost shouting, Tim cried, "I asked when you were born!"

Lippel fumbled for an answer. Then he turned to the policeman. "I don't have to answer his questions, do I?"

"You're under no legal obligation."

"See? I don't—"

"Why *not* answer? Do you have something to hide?"

"No, but—"

"Or have you forgotten?"

"I'm answering nothing. You want to cross-question me, you can get a lawyer and take me to court. I know my rights. You can't bullyrag me."

"All right, Lippel. You're sure that's your real name? You know how long you can go to jail if it isn't?"

"My name's Lippel, all right."

"How much is Brunner paying you?"

"Do I have to answer that?"

"No," said Constable Nevens. "All you have to answer are questions pertaining to the claim."

"See?" Lippel said to Tim, laughing with his whisky-barrel breath, showing a set of stained and rotting teeth.

"You plan to live up there?"

He looked at Nevens, Nevens nodded for him to answer, and he said, "Yes."

"How do you plan to get supplies?"

"You got to give me a right of way across your ground. I know my rights."

"How about you giving me right of way across *your* ground?"

"Not for no railroad!"

"How about it?" Tim asked, turning to the constable.

"The point is, you have him surrounded. You can't starve him out. In your case, it's possible to go around. You know very well you can't put a rail line across a man's land without—"

"Sure. How much will you take for a right of way?"

"It ain't for sale."

"That's what I thought. What if I paid you more than Brunner?"

"I don't admit that he's paid me a cent." Emboldened, Lippel went on. "Furthermore, I demand you get your rail line off my place."

"Not without a court order."

"How about it?" Lippel asked the constable.

"That's right. Not without a court order. The line is his property. You can't disturb it. Not a rail or a spike."

"What a hell of a thing that is! Chop up a man's fields, his own land, the only thing he's got in the world. How the government expects a man to make a living, go and chop up his farm with a railroad—"

Chipman and the constable both laughed at the ridiculous nature of his complaint. Then, disgusted, the constable said, "Come on, let's go."

Nevens saw him safely to the shanty. That evening he was back. He refused Tim's invitation to spend the night and went on, afoot, toward Talka.

The shanty was not livable, but Lippel made out until nightfall, and Tim's men, standing atop the engine cab, could see him crouched over an outside fire, trying to keep warm. In the morning the fire was out and there was no sign of him. There was a hopeful opinion current that he had frozen to death during the night, but he had not; he had slipped away by one of the side paths. His tracks led around Chipman, either to Talka or. to Vermilion. A day later he was on the ground again, this time with an escort of fourteen men, a group of saloon toughs that Brunner had recruited on the outside.

They had rifles, and they carried the rifles with them wherever they went. They barricaded the rail line with logs and went to work on the cabin, doing the bare minimum of work necessary to make it watertight. They set up a sheet-metal stove and cooked supper.· Later they went to work on a jug of whisky, and they could be heard whooping, singing, and fighting until long after midnight.

Lars Halseth said with satisfaction, "Sure, that's fine, they'll kill each other off pretty soon."

Young George Holman, who had been spying on them, came in frightened by his news and said, "There's a couple of 'em·ain't drunk. I sneaked clear up to the barricade, an' I *saw* 'em. I saw gun shine."

"You stay away from them, you crazy kid. I don't want you get killed. You leave all this to Tim. He'll know how to handle them saloon bums. You wait. Tim will fix up something geud and rough for them bums, by golly."

But Tim had nothing in mind. He did a lot of thinking and worrying and while he did it, logs kept coming down from Chilkao and piling high at the claim line. He hired an Indian driver and a string of huskies and mushed across the lake ice to Prince Albert. Nothing could be accomplished there, so he went on by train to Victoria. And all the while the logs were piled higher.

Chapter Twelve

Tim Chipman returned. It was evening, an early, gray evening, and he was walking around with his thick woolen socks catching the slivers of the floor, carrying a cup of coffee with him, when Mahon came down from the camp and remarked that Lippel must be getting his bellyful of his companions because he had sneaked out one of the back trails and headed in the direction of Talka.

"Where is he now?" Tim asked, motioning Mahon to the coffee.

"I don't know. I didn't even see him. Johnson was telling me." He looked up from the coffee, saw Tim putting on his boots, and said, "Hey, where you going?"

"I'd like to talk to Lippel—alone."

"Be careful you don't ring his rooster neck."

"I won't rough him up. I'll just talk to him."

He was too late to intercept Lippel. There was an inch of new snow covering the old, and he found Lippel's tracks coming down from the ridge and following the old railroad grade to Talka. He hurried to a trot, but Lippel was too far ahead. He reached Talka just in time to glimpse the man walking down one of the truck trails toward the wangan house.

Cursing his luck, Tim would have turned back to Chipman at that moment, but a speeder was coming along the track and he waited to see who its passengers were. It passed quite close, but its canvas shield was up, and it was only later, when it came to a stop by the shed, that he realized that Lynne Tilton and her father were on it. Talking and laughing in a voice that made magpie sounds through the cold was Frankie, the Japanese motorman.

Lynne and her father had been outside, to Vancouver and Victoria. Tim wanted to see her. The desire to see her was a force dragging him against his better judgment, but he resisted it. He did not want her to think he had been spying every night since she'd been gone, and so he turned and retraced his steps up the grade toward Chipman. His decision was one he regretted always.

Swiftwater Tilton had trouble when he got off the speeder. He cursed the speeder and the cold, but actually he was drunk.

Something was troubling him, and he had consumed a good deal more liquor than usual. He had been drunk in Vermilion, and Lynne had hoped that the trip by speeder through twenty-below cold would sober him, but it hadn't. He was still drunk, and he was in bad temper.

Frankie, the Japanese motorman, kept joking his best, pretending that Swiftwater wasn't drunk at all, until Swiftwater told him to be quiet.

"Sorry, Frankie," Lynne said to him when her father had maneuvered himself out of hearing.

She went to help him, but Swiftwater pulled roughly away from her.

"I don't need your help," he said. "What's the matter with you? Do you think I'm drunk?"

"I didn't say you were drunk."

"Well, all right. Because I'm not. I'm just stiffened from riding that damned speeder. Why in hell the Jap couldn't keep the windbreak mended!"

"Oh, Dad, Frankie is—"

"Frankie has been on the payroll too long. Trouble is he's too sure of his job. By God, if it was Brunner instead of me on that thing, he'd have the windbreak working. And don't try to talk me out of it. It's perfectly obvious to me how little I amount to around here."

He kept talking as he made it up the slightly rising ground to the company house. He stopped there and listened. The house was dark.

Lynne had hold of his arm. "Dad, come along home."

"No. *You* go home."

She saw there was no use trying to reason with him. She knew what was on his mind. He would go in there and start in on the company bottle. "All right," she said, and left him.

Swiftwater went inside and closed the door. It was dark. He groped down the hall, found his way through to the big room. He took off his coat and hung it up. The room was colder than he had expected. The Chinese flunky had let the fire go down.

He shouted, "Shen, come here!" but Shen did not answer.

He found the light switch and flicked it. Then he located the company bottle, and poured and downed a stiff one. The drink helped, but only a little. The stuff failed to buck him up as once it had.

He built up the fire. The effort tired him. It left him trembling. He stood with his back to the stove, waiting for warmth to come. He shivered and his teeth chattered. In the light of the naked electric bulb his skin looked white and curdled, like sour milk. He was puffy without being fat. His eyes kept watering, and tears ran from their outside corners. Swiftwater had been a strong man at one time, tall and whip-leather tough, a cruiser who could outlast a Cree Indian on the trail, but nobody would have guessed that now. Business failure and liquor had combined to ruin him.

He looked at the wall clock. Cold, coming in through the wall, had stopped it. He wondered where Brunner was. He had made up his mind to talk to Brunner, have it out with him, and he wanted him to come now, before he lost his nerve. He had taken on this extra load of whisky in preparation for having it out with Brunner. He thought of going to Brunner's room, but that always angered him.

A rap on the door startled him. He calmed himself by taking a deep breath. That wasn't Brunner, and he was glad.

"All right, come in," he said.

A man entered and paused apologetically, blinking in the light.

"Who in hell are you?" Tilton asked.

"Lippel. Frank Lippel."

"Oh, sure. I remember you. What do you want?"

"Just wanted to see the boss. It's O.K. with Mr. Brunner if I come here, long as I don't make a show of it. That's why I came after dark, so—"

"All right, Lippel. Come on in. I've been wanting to talk to you. Here, have a drink."

The invitation surprised and pleased him. They had run out of liquor up at the claim; at least those bastards said they had. You couldn't believe them. They didn't treat him very well. They were always causing him trouble behind his back, throwing steel wool in his blankets, filling his shoes full of water so they would be solid blocks of ice in the morning and then shouting,

"Fire, fire!" and laughing themselves limp when he tried to put them on. Of course, when *he* had a bottle he was a fine fellow and they helped him drink it up, but when one of them had a bottle it was different.

Lippel poured himself half a tumblerful and downed it. It was straight whisky, twelve years old, and he liked it.

"That's considerable different from the moose milk I been getting."

"Wood alcohol and chewing tobacco?"

"The boys made it, I don't know how. Southerland makes it. I think he mixes alcohol, water, and molasses. They take up a collection every week and send somebody out for alcohol. I put in my share but I never get my share of the liquor. They don't treat me very well out there, Mr. Tilton."

Swiftwater made a sympathetic sound. "By the way, what's your real name?"

Lippel was instantly on his guard. "Lippel. That's my real name."

Tilton was certain it was not. He did not like the man anyhow. He stepped back and, acting on sudden impulse, swung the back of his hand to Lippel's mouth.

It was not a hard blow, but it took Lippel so completely by surprise that he staggered, caught his heel on an edge of carpet, and fell to the floor. He caught himself on his elbows. The shock of falling had spilled a few strands of greasy hair over his eyes. He fingered the hair away, looked baffled for a moment, and whined, "What did you do that for?"

"I asked what your name was. People don't lie to me. When I ask a question I want the truth."

"I said—"

"I know what you said."

"Well, it's the truth. I'm Lippel. You ask Mr. Brunner. He knows what my name is. That's why he came to Nelson looking me up, because my name was Lippel. He told me he'd been almost a month running me down. He came up to me and said, 'Is your name Lippel?' and I said—"

"But you're not *the* Lippel."

He did not say anything to that. He crawled around to where Tilton could not reach him, and, using the table, got to his feet.

Tilton said, "You've never been in the Chilkoos Lake country before."

"Well, maybe I haven't, but that wasn't what you asked. You asked if my name was Lippel, and my name is Lippel."

"Where's the real Frank Lippel?"

"I don't know."

"Any relation?"

"Cousin."

"What if he shows up?"

"He won't."

"There's some legal advertising involved in this business, you know. He might see it."

"He'll read no legal advertising. He's dead." He moved around toward the bottle. He decided it was safe to pour another drink. He lifted it to his lips, and stopped. His eyes traveled to the door to one of the side rooms. Brunner was standing there. He probably had been standing there for some time. He knew Lippel had seen him, but still he made no sign, so Lippel made no sign, either. He drank the whisky. Then Brunner kicked something behind him, making a sound like someone just walking to the door, and he came inside.

"Oh, hello, Swiftie," he said to Tilton.

Tilton spun and said, "Hello!"

"I saw your light, wondered what the hell. Did you come in from Vermilion tonight?"

"Yes."

"It must have been urgent, come through on a night like this, on that speeder. Did Lynne come with you?"

Tilton nodded.

Brunner then turned his attention to Lippel. "What are you doing here?"

"Came down for some supplies."

"What the hell are you talking about? There's a ton of grub up there."

Lippel whined, "Well, I needed some tobacco, and I got to have a bottle of liquor. You ought to see how I get kicked around up there. Those strong-arm goons, they drank up every drop I had, and now they got a jug out in the bush, some I helped to pay for, and they drank up my share along with theirs, the dirty, cheating bastards, bunch of ax-handle stiffs, drinking my liquor, not playing fair, and playing tricks on me besides, filling my shoes with water, putting chopped hair in my tobacco—"

"All right, go on over to the wangan house and tell them what you need."

He waited for Lippel to get outside. He looked impatient and mean. His chin was set, and the muscles were big at the sides of his jaw.

"You two were having quite a talk," he said to Swiftwater.

"How much did you hear?"

Brunner shrugged.

"Why didn't you let me in on your scheme?"

"I don't care for your choice of words. Scheme, for instance. I don't scheme, I plan."

"You brought that dirty sneak up here, put him on the ground, on a claim that never belonged to him, real owner dead. How long do you think it'll be before Chipman's lawyers get at the truth? We can't get away with it."

"Go up there and have a look. Look at their logs stacking· up. We *are* getting away with it."

"Temporarily. Then what? He'll sue for everything you own."

"Tim won't sue anybody. He'll be broke. You don't cut much of a figure in court when you're broke."

"I don't like it."

It surprised Brunner that the man would stand up to him. He gave him his cold regard. He poured himself a drink and set it down without touching it.

Swiftwater went on. "I don't like it, and I won't associate myself with it."

"Pull out, then. Our agreement can be broken by mutual consent, and you have mine, right now, herewith. Pull out of the company and to hell with you. I plan to run Talka as I please."

"I will get out."

Brunner had expected him to curl up and play dead. The response surprised him. It took him aback for a second, and then it angered him. Fury, which he had never been able to control, darkened his face. It placed a tremble in his voice when he said, "You've been down to Vancouver, haven't you?"

"Yes."

"What were you doing?"

"It was private business."

"You have *private* business now. What the hell kind of a partnership do you call that?"

"You didn't consult me about Lippel."

"What were you doing in Vancouver?"

"I saw some old friends."

"Who?" Brunner shouted, advancing, and Tilton, answering in a shout, retreated before him.

"My private affair!"

"Who? Heuser and Long?"

"If I choose to see Heuser and Long, yes."

"You have it in your little scheming, drunken craw to pull your reserves out of the partnership and make a deal with them? *Private*, like you say. Private! Is that it? You think you could sell to Heuser and Long and leave me here with saws and no timber, holding the bag?"

He had Tilton cornered near the corner of the room. Tilton looked this way and that, but there was no escape. He was frightened, and fright showed in his eyes.

"I didn't say anything about selling to Heuser and Long. I said—"

Brunner laughed derisively.

"All I said was *if I chose*. I never double-crossed a man in my life. I'd have gone flat broke if it hadn't been for you, and I never denied it. I'm not now. But I still don't like that Lippel business. It will only be a question of time until Chipman finds out the truth."

"Chipman can't connect me with it. What proof does he have?"

"You're paying them."

"I never signed anything, no check, nothing. Everything has been cash." Brunner studied his face. He said in an easier tone, "I hope you haven't mentioned this to Lynne."

"Of course not."

"Good. Wouldn't want to trouble her. She might mention it to Chipman. I often wondered how he got wind of things. The Chilkao, for instance. And the little party I had arranged when he came for the engine. How did he find out about Dick Poole? Somebody could have told him. Somebody from here."

"Don't blame Lynne!"

"No?"

"No! She thinks you're all right. She takes your side. You're misjudged, the one who can do no wrong. You're rough, but you're honest. That's what Lynne thinks."

"And you don't like that. I'm good enough to save you from your creditors, but I'm not good enough to have for a son-in-law."

"I've said nothing. Lynne has her own life to live."

"You've always hated me, haven't you? 'Good old Croft' to my face, but privately you'd like to ruin me."

Swiftwater tried to get past, but Brunner shifted and blocked him.

"Let me by."

"No." Brunner grinned. "I've been thinking about Chipman and that Chilkao timber. You know, I don't believe Lynne told him, either. You know who I think it was?"

"Let me by!"

"It was you."

Swiftwater tried to duck around him. He almost succeeded. Brunner brought up his left arm, catching him beneath the chin, straightening him. When Tilton tried to go past on the other side, Brunner set his heels and brought up a right with all the smashing strength of his body.

The force of the blow almost lifted Tilton off the floor. He hit back and shoulders against the wall. His head snapped and hit the planks with a crack. He went down on folded legs and was limp with his head bent to one side, his eyes open and no sight in them.

Brunner did not stop. He pounced on the fallen man, seized him by his shirt, lifted him to dangling legs, and was ready to hit him again. He checked himself. Something in Swiftwater's limpness brought him to his senses.

"Swiftie!"

He got no answer. He tried to find out whether the man was breathing. Cursing under his breath, he carried him to a bench and laid him down. He got to one knee and listened for a heartbeat. He poured water on his face. There was no sign of life. That blow, the back of his head striking the wall, had killed him.

Brunner was sick and unnerved. He stood up. He looked around at the doors, at the windows. The doors were closed. The windows were thickly coated with frost. No one had seen him. No one but Lippel even knew they were alone together. Now if Lippel were dead— And he thought of reading somewhere that one killing leads to another.

But this wasn't a killing. It was an accident. The man had fallen and cracked his own head. Or perhaps it was partly the effect of whisky. A healthy man wouldn't have died from that.

Quiet, now. He could hear the snapping of wood in the stove. There was a creak outside, the complaint of packed snow under someone's weight. He listened. The sound was repeated and it died away. Someone going down to the mill. One of the stiffs on the night shift who had left his post and sneaked up to the wangan. He went to the door to make sure. He stood in the cold, looking outside. There was no one. He was about to turn away when he glimpsed Lynne Tilton coming from about fifty yards away.

Brunner wanted to go back and get the body out of sight, but he didn't have time. Besides, there was just a chance she had seen him standing there.

He went back for his mackinaw and cap and got to the door again in time to meet her.

"Lynne, what are you doing around this late?"

"Where's Dad?"

"Isn't he at the house?"

"No. He came here."

"Oh, sure. He was here, but he left. That must have been five minutes ago."

"Then you saw him?" She sounded relieved.

"I came in and found him talking to Lippel. He'll be at the house in a minute." He turned her around and started with her the way she had come. "I wish you'd come in. I was a little put out about it. Didn't you think I'd like to see you, after all the time you've been gone? Or don't I amount to anything any more?"

"Oh, Croft, you know you do! But Dad—well, you know—"

"Sure, I know. He's been drinking too hard. I'd have worried about you, coming up on the speeder."

"It wasn't bad."

"How were things in Vancouver?"

She made an almost guilty start. "Oh, he told you?"

"He said you'd been there."

"It was awfully expensive. I was the one who wanted to go. I thought it would help get him off the bottle."

Would you double-cross me, too? he was thinking. He dismissed that. He didn't want to believe that about her. He wanted to marry Lynne. He wanted that more than anything in the world. He walked with her, thinking about what had happened and trying to construct a way out. Finally such a way became clear to him.

"Now, Lynne, go up to the house and see if he's there. I'd like to talk with you, but it's too late. I want you to get some rest. Your dad made some threats, but it was just whisky talk and I give no weight to them. He's been drinking too—"

"What kind of threats?"

"Oh, he was all on edge. Lippel got him that way. Lippel ran out of whisky, and tonight he walked in on your dad."

"What happened?"

"Well, I wasn't there right at the moment, but Lippel gave your dad the idea he's an imposter, that I concocted the scene to keep Chipman from logging that Chilkao timber. Your dad said he was going to Chipman to tell all."

She cried, "You let him go on a night like this?"

"Lynne, you could never reason with your dad. How do you expect me to?"

She knew that that much was true; nobody could reason with him. She stood looking down at the front of her coat where the moisture of her breath had left a white coating of frost.

"Look at it my way, Lynne. What if I wouldn't let him go, kept him here by force? What would he believe? He'd think it was true, that I was afraid he'd peddle his crazy idea to Chipman. Now, he'll start out and get his fill of this weather in a quarter mile or so."

"We'd better follow him."

"Of course. I was going for a couple of the boys when I ran into you."

She believed him. She had never had any doubt about his feeling for herself or her father. As for the honesty of that Lippel business—well, that was something else.

She said, "Croft, what's going on up there? What about Lippel?"

"He's really Lippel. Word of honor. That's his real name. He took out that claim long ago. Good stand of timber on it, he has a legal right, and in case you didn't know, darling, your future husband has need of good timber. Losing the Chilkao really hurt me. *Us*. Chipman double-crossed us, and he got away with it. Chilkao, and then the train. Now he wants to use the train, and haul the very timber he cheated me out of across my land."

"Lippel's land."

"Well, we're buying it as soon as the title is cleared."

"Dad said you brought in some thugs from outside."

"Thugs? What a word! Guardsmen. Naturally I wouldn't hire first-class timberjacks to sit around up there and chew tobacco and drink whisky."

He walked with her along a path back of the wangan. The wangan was still lit, waiting for the night shift to come off, for the men liked to stop for a cup of coffee or a hot whisky. Through its walls they could hear Ax-Handle Ole's bellowing voice as he rolled dice, double or nothing, for drinks.

"Now, there's a sweet lad," Brunner remarked, just to be saying something.

"Why don't you send him up there?"

"To Lippel's? I need him here. He keeps the boys out of trouble."

He meant it for a joke, and she responded by laughing, but she still was worried about her father, and she kept looking uphill toward their house in the hope he would be there. Someone was moving between the light and a frosted window, but she knew it would be old Kawe Oseechekun, their Cree housekeeper.

Brunner guessed what was on her mind and said, "Well, if he isn't there, I'll send the boys out to track him. Stop worrying about him. He knows this country better than anybody in camp."

The snow had been shoveled, leaving some wooden steps bare. They led to a narrow snow shed along the front of the house. She expected Brunner to leave her at the door, but he came inside with her.

He said, laughing, "Why, Lynne, you act as though you wanted to get rid of me. After all, we haven't seen each other for three weeks."

"Oh, Croft, I didn't want to get rid of you." Ordinarily

she would have been glad to see him, but tonight she was worried. "Dad!" she called.

"No, he not here," the Indian woman answered.

"It's all right, Lynne," he said, getting a grip on her arms.

"Yes, I shouldn't worry. Good night, Croft."

He did not go. "Everything's the same between us, isn't it?"

"Of course."

"I'm going to marry you, Lynne." When she did not answer, he said gently, "You heard me."

"Yes, only I'm so tired, and worried."

He was thinking that Tim Chipman had been away to Vancouver on that Lippel business.

"Did something happen—on your trip?"

"No. Croft, send them out after him, will you?"

"Of course."

He said good night to her and went outside.

Chapter Thirteen

AFTER HE WAS gone, Lynne stood by the door, listening. She had the feeling that he was just on the other side, also listening, and it frightened her. Then she heard the squeak of snow under his weight as he went down the path, and she took a deep breath and felt better.

"Kawe," she said.

The Indian woman, at the top of the stairs, said, "Sure."

"Lay out my woolens and parka."

Kawe got them and Lynne dressed quickly. She looked very small in the oversize parka with its wolverine hood circling her head. She left by the rear door because she did not wish to meet Brunner. She waded through the deep snow and found one of the truck trails, the one she expected her father to take in the direction of Chipman. New snow had fallen; no one had been along it for several hours.

She turned back and looked for other routes. She went to the railroad track and found the new impressions left by Lippel and Tim. She started following Tim's returning tracks, only to realize, after a hundred yards or so, that these were not her father's, these were left by a snow boot while her father wore hard heels, and these were at least an hour old, sprinkled over by light crystals of frost.

She turned back. She did not know where to go next. She went to the company house. There was no light there, so she walked on to the wangan. Women were not as a rule welcomed at the wangan, but she opened the door. Old Torgorson, the crippled timberjack who ran the place on commission, was there alone with a Swedish-language newspaper spread before him on the bar.

He saw her and said, "Yah, it's all right, you coom in har any time you like, miss. You want package cigarettes, anything, you coom right in."

"I was looking for my dad."

"I haven't seen him. By golly, I ain't seen old Swiftwater in two-three week."

She thanked him and turned to go back outside. She

remembered that Ax-Handle Ole had been there. She wondered if Brunner had sent him to look for her father.

"Did Mr. Brunner come here for Ax-Handle Ole?"

"Yah."

"Did he say anything about looking for my dad?"

"No. What's wrong? Your papa lost?"

"I don't know."

She decided to go to Brunner's room. Once outside, however, she noticed a light in the bunkhouse where Ole stayed. She went there instead. She knocked, and after a considerable delay Ole inched the door open and peeped out at her.

"Hah?" he said, surprised. He looked more than surprised. He looked frightened.

"What are you doing here?"

"Just har."

"Aren't you out looking for my dad?"

He stared at her in his dumb way and it infuriated her. She cried, "Why aren't you out looking for him?"

"No! I ain't going to do it!"

"Is he in there with you?" She didn't know what gave her that idea.

"No!"

"He is. Why don't you open the door? You're hiding him in there."

Ole stepped back and opened the door—an old plank door that dragged on the rough floor. He stepped back so she could see. It was a deep, low, filthy room lit by a brownish kerosene lamp. Cards, old socks, underwear, and pulp magazines strewed the floor.

"See, he not har."

"Dad!" she called, knowing now that Ole had been telling the truth.

"You go away noo."

She noticed that Ole had been filling a war sack with his clothing.

"Where were you going?"

"Goin' to quit," he muttered.

"Why?"

"This is free coontry."

"Why are you quitting?"

"Just sick of workin' har."

"You sounded happy enough down at the wangan an hour or so ago."

"Goin' to Vermilion, maybe Prince Albert, get yob on halibut trooler."

Unseen and unheard, Brunner had come up behind her. He spoke and she spun around, uttering a little cry of surprise.

"Lynne, what are you doing here?"

"I'm looking for Dad."

"Here?"

"I thought you had Ole out looking for him. I saw his light on so I came to see."

"That's right, why isn't he out looking for him? I'll take care of it. Lynne, you go on back to the house. What the devil! Where have you been?"

"Around. I tried to find his tracks. I—"

"Were you down to the office?"

"No. Do you think he might—"

"I just came from there. I thought I heard someone walking along the porch." He turned her around and took her toward the house. "Now, everything will be all right. Believe me. I'll take care of it. I'll find your dad."

"What about Ole?"

"I'll see about Ole. And I'll get some of the other boys. Now go home and take off that trail outfit. You look like you were headed for Fort Resolution."

Brunner made certain she went all the way home. He then went back to the bunkhouse, went inside, closed the door, and stood with his shoulders against it, looking at Ax-Handle Ole.

"Where are you going?"

"Leavin'."

"You mean you're quitting?"

"Yah."

"What did you tell her?"

"Nothin'. I didn't tall her a damn thing, I yust—"

"You said you were quitting, though."

Ole did not answer. He was wary of the man in front of him. He kept stealing looks this way and that, judging the room, looking for some means of escape. There were a couple of windows, but they were tiny, pegged fast, and frozen besides. There was a door at the other end, but years had passed since it had been opened, and things were heaped in front of it.

"Did she ask why you were quitting?"

"Yah."

"What'd you tell her?"

"I didn't tall her damn thing, yust like I said before. I yust said I was pullin' out for Vermilion. I tall her I was gettin' goddamn geud and sick of havin' everybody call me labor fink, call me names behind my back, spying on my friends, strong-arm stuff, all that."

"Nothing about her father?"

"No!"

"You're not quitting, Ole, so get your stuff out of the bag and put it back where it belongs."

"Quittin' tonight."

Brunner stayed where he was, his back against the door, and he shook his head. His face had undergone a change. Anger, as always, had put the savage stamp on it, making his cheeks hollow and the sides of his jaw large. Working slowly, he unbuttoned his mackinaw and took it off.

"Har, noo!" said Ole, retreating beyond the war sack.

Brunner came forward. "No, Ole. You're not quitting. You collected double pay too long. No man collects double pay from me and then leaves when the going gets rough."

Ole was frightened, but he had set his mind on going and he was obstinate. He shook his massive head. "I'm goin'."

"No. Unpack the war sack."

"Took double pay, yah. Fightin' man, yah. Big strong faller, whip five-sax men at one time, fists, hobnails, but don't have nothing to do with other stuff. Don't have nothin' to do with murder."

Brunner was a stride away, holding himself very taut. The word "murder" snapped the leash of his restraint. He came forward, arms long and loose, his fists doubled.

Ole did not retreat. He parried a left and right. He moved to the middle of the room. He started a haymaker. Brunner came inside it, taking its force on his back. He hesitated an instant as Ole tried to recover his balance, and he swung a right like a sledge to the point of Ole's jaw.

Ole reeled. He was wobbly but he did not fall. He went backward, trampled a stool to pieces, both arms in front of him. He hit the wall. He hit it so hard the whole house shook and some magazines on a shelf were dislodged and came showering over him to the floor. He rebounded and seemed about to go down, but he did not. He stopped in a crouched position, still able to focus his eyes, and his eyes were on Brunner.

Brunner came after him, slow and sure of himself. He said, "You're working for me, Ole."

"Goin' to quit!"

Ole had the advantage of reach. He thrust far out with a left and kept Brunner away. He moved around the room, jabbing with the left, and tried again with the haymaker. They slugged toe to toe with Brunner unable to get another clean shot at him. A haymaker drove Brunner back, an upswinging left spun him against one of the bunks that lined the wall.

Ole thought he had him at his mercy. He roared and charged in, ready to smash him down and trample him.

Brunner was ready. He moved with his back against the bunks. He made him miss. He came around in a half pivot, set his hobs in the rough plank floor, waited until Ole turned to follow, and came up with a left and right that dropped Ole like a steer under the hammer.

Ole hit the floor with his legs bent under him. Holding to the edge of a bunk with one hand, Brunner vaulted and drove a foot to the side of Ole's head.

The big Swede hit flat on his back with his arms out. Brunner came on, trampling him. He wore logger boots with oak-leather soles half an inch thick, frozen from the snow, armored with hobnails. He trod on him, tearing flesh from his head and his ribs. He stepped back and kicked him repeatedly, kicked and kept kicking until fatigue stopped him.

It might have killed an ordinary man, but Ole was not quite unconscious. Panting, Brunner stepped back. He supported himself on one of the bunks, watching Ole drag himself to hands and knees.

"All right, get out," Brunner said between gasps. When the words failed to register, he shouted, "Get out!"

"Yah."

Ole remained for the better part of a minute with

his head hanging down and blood running from his torn ears and face and from inside his mouth to soak the front of him and drip on the floor. Finally, with the help of a bench and the table, he reached a standing position. "Yah," he said again.

Without hat or mackinaw he reeled to the door. He jerked at it a dozen times before he got it open. He tripped and fell headlong on the frozen path. He crawled on hands and knees as Brunner came to the door and threw his war sack and extra clothing after him.

"Wait!"

Ole stopped. He waited to hear what Brunner had to say, his head down, his hair touching the snow.

"Can you understand what I'm saying?"

"Yah."

"Get out. Stay away. Don't ever let me see you again. Never. Don't stay in this country. Go back to the States. If I ever see you again, no matter where, I'll kill you. Do you hear that? I'll kill you!"

Chapter Fourteen

Ax-Handle Ole crawled beyond the outbuildings. He got to his feet. He managed to stay on his feet and walk. He walked and kept walking with no idea where he was going. When he became dizzy he sat down in the snow. His right ear continued to bleed. The blood turned to ice, and broke off, and then it bled again. Brunner's hobs had cut the ear almost in two. He tried to mend it by holding the two segments together. Finally he got his wits about him and looked around to see where he was. He found he had been following one of the truck roads to the logging camps.

He sat down and used snow to clean some of the blood off his face. The snow pained him, it was rough on his cut face, but he felt better when it was over. He thought of his war sack. He decided to go back after it. Everything he owned, money, clothes, watch, and stickpin, was in it. He would keep his eyes open.

He slunk in by one of the back trails. The war sack was where he had left it. He got it and hurried off into the shadows. He intended to go to Vermilion. When he reached the railroad he reconsidered. At best his mind did not function rapidly, so reconsidering took no little time.

Brunner had killed Tilton. Ole knew that because Brunner had wanted him to get rid of the body. Only two people knew about it—Brunner and himself. If Ole were dead, then only Brunner would know about it. Brunner would like that, because murder was a serious thing. They would hang Brunner, yes, even Brunner, if they found out about it. Ole might talk and get him hanged. The question was, why hadn't Brunner killed him? The answer to that was that then Brunner would have to get rid of *two* bodies, and Ole's would be a big one to get rid of. But down at Vermilion was Burgess, a man Brunner could trust. Brunner might phone Vermilion and tell him to keep his eye out for Ole and have an accident happen to him. All these thoughts slowly worked their way through the plodding cells of Ax-Handle Ole's brain.

He felt helpless, not knowing which way to turn, having to make up his own mind, not having anyone to tell him what to do. So it was natural for him to turn to Brunner's chief enemy.

He walked toward Chipman.

It was still dark, although there was a hint of gray morning light rising over hills and forest when he reached the settlement. A couple of buildings were lighted, wood sparks came from a chimney, and a slight breeze carried to his nostrils the odor of frying ham.

He knew there would be a sentry posted. He decided to sneak in by way of the river. He waded through snow and fought brush. He made a great commotion, but nobody hailed him, and he crossed the clearing unnoticed.

He could hear voices—rough Scandinavian voices. Some of the men had just come off shift and were waiting for what would be their supper; others, just going on, would call it breakfast. In the background a concertina was playing with a windy wheeze. Ole stood outside the door and listened. That tune, by golly, it made him almost want to cry. It was a tune he had not heard since the old days in Nort' Dakota. He stood listening, his great, bruised face slack and forlorn. And now a Swedish voice was singing,

> "I bane workin' hard for you, Steena Stone,
> I bane workin' hard for you
> All around a threshin' crew,
> Yust bane workin' hard for you, Steena Stone."

Ole rapped at the door. When the sound went unnoticed, he rapped harder. Now the concertina stopped on a dying chord and a man called, "Yah, coom in, what the hell?"

Ole opened the door. Hesitant, he moved inside. He stood blinking as the men stared at him, realizing who he was.

"Well, knock me down," somebody cried, "if it ain't the Ax-Handle 'isself."

"Yah."

"Har, noo!" said the Swede with the concertina. He was an elderly man with a gray mustache under-stained by snoose. "If you're lookin' for trouble, you come to the right place. You yust find out—"

"Ain't lookin' for trouble," said Ole. "By golly, I had trooble enough already for one night."

"Yipes!" shouted another one. "Look at the face on 'im! 'E *has* been havin' his troubles. Just look at that case of lumberjack's measles!"

Lars Halseth heard the excitement and came in from another part of the building. "Well, what do you want?"

"I coom har look for yob."

"Here? We don't hire finks. We don't hire scabs, either."

"Ain't no fink. Ain't scab, neither. I coom down har to yoin the union."

Lars looked him over. His face was still smeared with blood. Here and there the blood had gathered in blackened chunks. His face had had time to swell, and it was lumpy and lopsided. His eyes were swollen shut and he had to keep his head tilted back a trifle in order to see.

"Good Lord!" Lars said admiringly. "What a yob!" Somebody sure did work you over. Who was it?"

"Brunner. He beat hell out' of me. He get me down and yoomp all over me."

"And then he fired you?"

"Yah."

"Why?"

Ole became obstinate. "Ain't talkin'. Not without you give me yob."

Lars perhaps suspected that this was some sort of deadfall. The state of Ole's face reassured him, but he was suspicious anyway.

Ole said, "Ain't talkin' no more. You take me to Tim Chipman. Tim Chipman will give me a yob and I'll be plenty geud man, by golly."

Tim Chipman, who had preceded Ole by about three hours, was in his bunk asleep. He sat up and cursed when Lars stuck his head inside and called his name.

"Visitor," Lars said.

Without reason, he expected it to be Lynne, and he sprang out of bed in a hurry.

"Where is she?"

"*She?* What you got on your mind, kid? This ain't

no woman. This is Ax-Handle Ole, lookin' for a yob."

Tim stood barefoot on the cold floor and stared at the huge, hulking form that had followed Lars through the door.

"That?"

"It's Ax-Handle Ole, all right," Lars said happily. "Look at that face! A beauty, hey? He's really been run through the meat grinder. By golly, that boss man down at Talka really made cube steak out of him."

"He yoomp on me," said Ole.

"Brunner?"

"Yah."

Tim lit the lamp in order to see him better. He pulled on his wool socks, fastened them with safety pins to the long underwear he had been sleeping in, and got his pants on, all the while appreciating the beautiful state of Ole's face.

"What was it about?"

"I quit."

"Why?"

"Yust sick of that place. Sick of being fink, have everybody walk off when I coom around, won't even shoot dice wit' me, so I say I quit, want my pay, and he knock me down, yoomp on me."

"What did you do, just take it?"

"We had pretty geud fight." Ole thrust out his hands and made fists of them. His fingers were the size of bananas, and it was hard for him to bend them. His knuckles had all been knocked out of place, and they were inflamed and skinned. "Yah. I get him a coople of geud licks, too."

"So you want a job."

"Yah, Bane geud fighter. Timberyak, too. Willin' to yoin the union."

"That's up to the boys and Lars. How about it, Lars? Can you use a timber bucker?"

"I'll hitch him up with that old bay mare and use him to haul cars on the railroad."

Tim thought the big fellow was holding something back. The suspicion grew stronger a couple of days later when he heard that Swiftwater Tilton had wandered away from Talka and was still missing. Then one afternoon young George Holman hunted him at Chilkao camp to tell him that a man's body had been found, covered by an inch of new snow, across the river from the old Chipman mill.

"Tilton?" Tim asked, but George didn't know.

They took a short cut and reached the place about dark. A lantern showed through the trees.

"That it?" Tim asked.

George said, "I guess so. I wasn't there, all the way. I didn't see the body."

George didn't want to look at the dead man now, either, and Tim, understanding it, said, "It's all right. I don't need you now. You can stay back."

"Naw. I'll come."

There were more lights, the twin headlights of a car. It was a Model A Ford with snow tracks that had come down from Talka. Shadows moved against the lights and he could hear voices.

"Wait!" a man cried from the timber close by the trail. "Who is it?"

"Chipman."

"Tim Chipman?" The man came into view with a rifle over his arm. "Just a second," he said, courteously enough, and he called, "Hey, here's Chipman now."

"All right." Tim recognized Brunner's voice.

He heard Steve Riika say something, too, and he supposed there were several others from his own camp.

He walked in among them. The snow had all been tracked and cross-tracked.

"Hello, there," Brunner said, his big form, very sure of itself, silhouetted against the headlamps.

"Hello, Croft," Tim answered. "Who is it? Swift-water?"

"Yes."

"Dead?"

"Yes."

"Does Lynne know?"

Brunner made a motion, pointing her out. She was on the far side of the snowmobile. Beyond her, on a tarp, lay a man's body, frozen stiff with snow in his hair.

"Hello, Tim," the girl said.

He walked to her. She was wearing her parka. It made her seem very small. He wanted to tell her how sorry he was, but the words that came from his lips didn't seem like much.

"I guess he was coming up here to see you," she said. "If I'd only known. I heard he was missing, but—"

"It wasn't anybody's fault. We tried to follow him and couldn't. He must have left along one of the truck tracks and got off somewhere. I don't know."

"When?"

She named the night, the night he knew it was. He kept thinking about Ax-Handle Ole.

He looked down on the dead man's face. It was bruised. The bruises were not easy to distinguish by the reflected light of the headlamps, but they were there.

Tim said, "Did he say he was coming to my place?"

"He didn't tell me."

"He told *me*," said Brunner.

"Oh."

Tim's tone made Brunner say, "Now listen here. If you mean to indicate—"

"I don't indicate things, Croft, I *say* things. I see things, too. Those bruises, for instance."

Brunner said bitterly, "The crazy punk kids you have guarding your place! He ran into one of 'em is what happened. Sure, down here, off the trail, wallowing through the bushes, and one of them slugged him."

"Like they slugged Ax-Handle Ole, I suppose."

"Wait!" Lynne got between them. "Don't fight. Don't quarrel about it. He wasn't murdered. He had been drinking. I'll tell you the truth, Tim, because everyone else knows it anyway. He was drunk. He was staggering drunk. He probably tripped and fell to get those bruises. Stop trying to make it out worse than it was."

Brunner got his arm around her. "Of course, Lynne." He led her away. "Everything will be all right. Get in the car, now. We'll go back to camp. Everything will be all right."

Chapter Fifteen

Tim Chipman returned to camp, got a lantern, and returned to the place. Everyone was gone. All around the snow was trodden, and he walked in wider and wider circles trying to pick up Tilton's tracks, but wherever he went new tracks obliterated the old ones. After a fruitless three hours he returned to camp. Next morning he hunted out Ax-Handle Ole.

He got Ole into a corner and said, "You knew about it all the time, didn't you?"

"No!" Ole cried, wagging his head from side to side, watching him with scared eyes.

"Why, you yellow—"

"Ain't yellow. Whip damn saloonful of Irishmen. Have plenty guts. Just don't know nothin' about this stuff."

"What happened? Did Brunner kill him? He did, didn't he? They got to quarreling about the Chilkao timber, and Brunner hit him, isn't that it?"

"I don' know."

"Or were they quarreling about Lynne?"

"I tall you—"

"What did Brunner do—ask you to carry him up here? But you were more scared of the body than you were of Brunner, and so you got into that battle with him."

"I yust quit. I told you truth all the time—*I yust quit.*"

"Maybe you killed him!"

"No!"

Tim could not decide whether he was lying or not. His face, still somewhat puffed, served as a mask, and Ole didn't have the type of face that showed much, anyway.

"You'd like to run out on me now, wouldn't you?"

"No. I stick to my job."

"Like hell! We've furnished the raw meat for your face, and now you'd like to get over the hump to Chinook Inlet. Well, don't try it."

Ole stared at him.

"Let me tell you, Ole, if you make a run for it, that'll be just proof in my eyes that you're guilty. If I wake up some morning and find your bunk empty, I'll swear out a paper for your arrest."

Ole looked very sick now. He sat down on a bunk and held his head in his hands. "Ain't goin' nowhere. Wish I never coom to this country. Wish I was back in Nort' Dakota."

Afterward, Tim said to Steve Riika, "I know when that big goon will remember all about that night down in Talka—he'll remember it the day Croft Brunner dies."

Steve said, "That might not be a bad idea."

"Don't talk like that. Anyway, I want to lick him and leave him in shape so he'll remember it."

"Not Brunner. You'll get it like Clay, unless you get him first. I tell you, the only way to beat that Brunner is to kill him."

A mounted police corporal came to investigate Swiftwater Tilton's death, but he did not establish it as murder. He visited Talka and Chipman and went home again. Hearing from the policeman that the funeral was scheduled for the following day, Tim got his dress clothes out of his war sack, where they had been since the autumn before, pressed them, and walked to Talka. The policeman had been in error. Tilton had been buried, with simple prayers, the day before.

Tim had walked openly into camp. The day had turned warm, and men stood outside in their shirt sleeves, watching him. He saw Dick Poole, Shorty Garrity, and a couple of others whom he recognized. If Brunner was around he did not show himself.

Feeling conspicuous, not only because of who he was, but because of his dress shoes, suit, and overcoat, an almost unknown garment in that country, he walked quickly up a side path to Tilton's house to offer condolences. Lynne opened the door almost before he had the chance to rap.

"Come in, Tim," she said, as if there were nothing in the least uncommon about his being there.

"I wanted to attend the services. The mountie said it would be today. I guess I'm late."

"It was yesterday. But thanks for coming."

She really meant it, he knew she did, and now he was glad he had come, dress shoes, overcoat, and all.

She showed him to the living room, small but well furnished with rugs, drapes, some beautiful old mahogany cabinets, and an overstuffed set. After so many months in his big, bare, cold quarters at Chipman, the room seemed confining and too hot.

"Sit down, Tim," she said, and took his hat.

"You're going to stay on?"

The question surprised her. "Why, of course. What else would I do?"

"I was just trying to start a conversation."

"Yes, I have to hold up Dad's end. It's my life, too. Dad and Croft had the loosest kind of partnership."

"You inherit the timber?"

"Don't try to buy it from me, Tim."

He laughed and said, "What with?"

"Well, you know what people were saying, that Dad intended to sell out, pull his reserves out of the partnership. There was no truth to it, of course. We wouldn't have owned a stick if it hadn't been for Croft."

She had been telling herself that over and over, Tim thought, explaining to herself why she had to remain loyal, trying to tell herself that she was still in love with Brunner, too, and that she wanted to marry him.

He changed the subject. They talked about small things, about mutual acquaintances from the old days.

The Indian woman came in carrying tea, English biscuits, and a pitcher of condensed milk. He drank his tea straight, and so hot it left scales on his tongue.

When the woman was gone he said, "Your dad didn't feel quite so grateful to Croft. He felt he'd given more than his share. That's why he tipped me off about the Chilkao."

"He did tell you, then?"

Tim nodded.

"I always thought so, of course."

"And Croft—did he always think so?"

"I don't know." She reached and laid her hand on his arm. "Tim, you shouldn't hate him so."

"Hate Croft? I don't hate him. I just loathe his guts."

"The policeman was up to see you, wasn't he?"

"Yes."

"Did he think Dad met foul play up there?"

"He had it in the back of his mind, but he didn't come right out and say it. He just did a lot of inquiring about my sentries, who they were, what their orders were, things like that."

"Croft didn't accuse you. I hope you didn't accuse him, either."

"I didn't. I wouldn't accuse him unless I could prove he was guilty."

"Oh, Tim, you know he wouldn't harm my dad."

"How about Ax-Handle Ole?"

"What about him?"

"Brunner worked him over pretty well that same night. Got him down and kicked him in the head. Do you happen to know why?"

"I don't believe it. Ole left here of his own free will."

"He's at my camp now. He looks like he went through one of those jaw crushers up on Porcupine."

"He had lots of enemies. How do you know it was Croft?"

"Well, Croft is man enough to do it."

"Let's not talk about it any more."

He could see that she was determined to believe her father's death an accident. He couldn't blame her; the tragedy would seem less that way.

"Just one more question—who saw your father last?"

"Lippel, I think."

"Lippel?" He took new interest.

"You couldn't suspect him—that mouse."

"Rat."

"No, just a mouse."

"What's his real name?"

"It's Lippel. And that's his claim, legally. You're wasting your money having your lawyers investigate him."

He dropped the subject. They talked on for another hour, about Vancouver, about hockey, about acquaintances. Old Kawe had come quietly into the dining room and stood until Lynne took notice of her through the arch.

"Yes, Kawe?"

"He come pretty soon," she said.

"Oh, yes." A furrow appeared between Lynne's eyebrows. "Croft," she said to Tim.

"Business conference?" Tim asked, trying to give it a sprightly sound but not getting the tautness out of his voice.

"He asked to have his cook prepare dinner and bring it over here. He likes to do things like that. I don't mind, of course." She glanced to make sure that Kawe was gone. "The food is better. Kawe is a darling, but the Crees were never very famous as cooks."

"Are you going to marry him?" he asked abruptly.

It took her by surprise. She stood and stared at him for a few seconds without breathing.

"Are you?" he repeated.

Apparently she did not know the answer herself. So, instead of answering directly, she said, "Why shouldn't I?"

"Because you're not in love with him. I've seen girls in love. You're not in love."

"You're an expert on that now!"

"I don't need to be."

He took hold of her shoulders. She seemed very fragile. It seemed within his power to crush her in his hands.

She started to say something and changed her mind. She looked up at him. She should have been fighting away from him, but she wasn't. He drew her hard against him and kissed her. He kissed her several times as she gave herself willingly. Then, suddenly, she was a bundle of strength, twisting away from him.

She whispered, "No, Tim! Get out of here!"

Kawe came running. They could hear the jarring thud of her weight in moccasins.

"Anything trouble?"

"No," said Lynne. She was flushed, and her hair had come undone across her shoulders. "Get Mr. Chipman's hat."

He took it. He walked to the door. He stood in the open door, smiling in at her.

"You won't marry him," he said. "I know you won't."

Chapter Sixteen

He noticed how much longer the days were getting. A bluish haze had settled, but it was still daylight. There was a wind from the south. The wind was raw and piercing, but from dampness rather than cold, for the snow had a slick, wet feeling underfoot.

"Chinook," he said.

It would take the snow down, there would be small torrents in the gulches, and it would freeze again. There would be cold weather yet, maybe thirty-below weather, but for a few days only; the back of the water was broken. That meant it was now or never for the Chilkao timber.

It was dark when he got home, and he missed the special message broadcast over Station CJFA in Vancouver, but Steve had listened in for him.

"No, Tim," Steve said. "No word from those damn lawyers."

Tim relieved his feelings by cursing a little.

Steve said, "We got to do something. That's a Chinook wind blowing."

"I know."

"We got to get those logs to the ice. When that river goes we'll have flood for a week. Maybe only three-four days. If—"

"You're not telling me a thing."

"Well, yah."

Steve was dissatisfied. He stood around, wanting to remonstrate, and then stalked off to be by himself. Steve wasn't the only one who was dissatisfied. Tim could feel it all through the camp. There was talk again that the outfit was going broke. The mountain of logs accumulating at the Lippel boundary was visible proof that the outfit would go broke.

Tim said to Steve, "We'll give those lawyers another week." He stopped Steve from arguing: "Now wait! I've thought it all out. I know how we've been held up, I know how many logs are there, and I know how fast we can haul them to the river. I got the Chilkao, didn't I? I got the railroad and engine. Well, trust me to do the rest of it."

He sounded confident—a hell of a lot more confident than he really was. Under his cocky exterior he felt sick at the delay.

Finally his message came through. His lawyers said it was no use, they could do nothing until late summer, perhaps the following autumn.

"And not then," said Steve Riika when he heard. "Well, now what?"

Tim laughed and looked at his work-scarred hands with their broken nails. "We couldn't get through *with* the law, so we'll have to get through without it."

"Mountie will be here in two days."

"That depends."

"On what?"

"On whether it really is Lippel's claim. I've been thinking a lot about this, putting myself in Brunner's shoes, thinking what I'd do if I were Brunner. Say he's running a bluff. He won't stand up there and fight in defense of a legal fake."

"His name is Lippel. I told you about old George. He knew him down in Kamloops."

"Hell is full of Lippels. Is he the one and original Lippel? That claim dates to a long time back. I don't think he's old enough."

Tim got his revolver and dropped it in his mackinaw pocket.

"What you going to do?" Steve asked, alarmed.

"I'm going to pay Lippel a visit."

Tim did not ordinarily like to go armed for fear a gun might lead to more trouble than it would solve, but this was a special case. He would be far outnumbered, and the revolver would run a good bluff. It would scare hell out of Lippel, and that was what he wanted.

He walked out into the dark, under the hazy stars. He followed the track. It had been shoveled clear of snow to a point about two hundred yards short of the Lippel boundary; from there a path led on, but he did not follow it. He waded knee-deep in melting snow and reached the timber. Darkness closed in on him so he had to grope his way. He walked for what seemed a long time, sometimes through brush that held the snow lightly, making it hip-deep.

He stopped suddenly at the sound of a voice. A man

had spoken; the voice seemed to be right beside him.
A second man said something. They were talking to each
other about twenty-five yards away. Sentries, the watch-
men always posted near the barricade.

He moved on slowly through underbrush, and found
the path they had been following between the lookout
post and the cabin. Wet to the knees, he followed it.

After forty or fifty yards, he saw light in two brownish
squares—the cabin windows.

They had repaired the cabin, but it was too small to
accommodate them all, so they had built a long lean-to
with its back against a knoll. Pieces of stovepipe were
poked through the lean-to roof in a couple of places,
but no smoke came from them tonight.

Here again men were talking. It was warm enough so
they could lie around outside. He could not make them
out. He could see nothing except the light, a ruddy lamp
glow through the smoked-up windowpanes.

He stopped at the edge of a small clearing that once
had been a cabbage patch. The original Lippel had built
a pole fence around it, and part of the fence still stood,
but only an upright here and there showed above the
snow.

He waded again, sometimes to his armpits. He found
footing on the old fence and climbed over it. He sank
deep again. He was now somewhat to the rear of the
cabin, and hidden from it by the lean-to. He located
another path, followed it for a few steps, waded through
more snow, and reached the cabin, stopping in safety
beneath the shadow of the eaves.

He listened. The men were out of view. He examined
that side of the log building. There were no windows,
but there was a door made of split rail, warped and
recently mended with slats from apple boxes. It was
not much of a job. Pieces of gunny sack were wadded
into the cracks, and still light came through. He peeped
through one after another of the holes without being
able to see much of the interior, only bits of the far
wall, a table leg, and part of what looked like a bunk.

From the lean-to a man shouted, "Hey, Lip, do you
hear me?" He was yelling at Lippel, and Lippel, inside
the cabin, moved and seemed to be listening. "Hey,
Lip, I'll raise that to fifty cents, cash money."

Tim knew that Lippel was just on the other side of

the door. It was his guess that Lippel had locked himself in as protection against those strong-arm goons, who obviously disliked him.

"Lip, fifty cents! That's a good price for moose milk. What do you say, Lip?"

"How many times I got to tell you I got no liquor?" Lippel answered.

They kept shouting back and forth, the toughs offering to slip their money under the door, and Lippel insisting he was out of liquor. Gently Tim tried the door. It did not move. It was spiked fast on the inside. He stepped back, waited until Lippel was in the act of talking, and came forward shoulder first, bursting inside.

Lippel spun to face him, reaching for a rifle against the wall, but Tim was ready for that. He had only to change the direction of his momentum, and he carried the smaller man with him to the wall.

Lippel half fell between the wall and the wood box. He still had hold of the rifle, but he could not bring it around. He opened his mouth and started to shout, but Tim choked off the sound with a forearm pinning his throat to the wall.

They remained in that position for a few seconds, Lippel staring at him with protruding yellowish eyes, his mouth open. He breathed with a wheezing sound through the small passage left through his windpipe.

"Going to yell to 'em?" Tim asked.

He did not get an answer, of course. Lippel could not even make a negative sign with his head. He could only stare and try to make himself understood with his eyes.

"You bring 'em here and I'll snap your neck."

He let him go. He rocked back and took the rifle. Lippel stayed where he was, getting his breath. Finally he felt strong enough to whine, "What are you looking for?"

Tim moved the rifle. He went to the front door to bar it, but it was already barred. "Don't you get along with the boys?"

"Those bastards! You don't know what I put up with, denned up with those sons—"

"Well, you should come down to Chipman."

"I know it. I know I should. I *would* have, too, a

couple of times, if I could have got away. They practic-
ally hold me a prisoner here. I got nothing against you.
I took this place back with no thought of harming you.
I was only so damned broke, and this the only piece of
property I had in the world, after a life of hard work,
scrimping and saving—"

"Only you're not the real Lippel."

"I am! Yes, as honest as I stand here—"

"You're not old enough. You weren't ten years old
when this claim was taken out. Now, don't lie to me
or you *will* get your neck broke. Where is the real
Lippel?"

"Damn it, that's what *he* asked."

"Who?"

"Him." He wished now he'd never mentioned it. He
wanted to lie, but Tim was watching him, and he was
scared that Tim would know he was lying. "That old
fellow, what's-his-name, Swiftwater, the fellow that
died."

"When did you see him? You saw him the night he
disappeared, didn't you?"

"No, I—"

"His daughter told me you did."

If there was any resistance left in Lippel, this took
it out of him. "Yes, I saw him. But I don't know anything about what happened to him. I had nothing to do
with it. He was all right when I left him."

"Alone with Brunner?"

"Yes."

"What was the trouble between Brunner and Ole?"

"I don't know. Just what the boys said at the wangan,
that they got in a fight, that Brunner got mad when Ole
tried to quit."

"Whose claim was this?"

"Lippel, like I said."

"Any relation?"

"Cousin."

"Where is he?"

"Dead."

"He abandoned it?"

Lippel nodded.

Tim said, "I can see that we're going to get along.
From here on, you'll get along with me better than you
will with Brunner. You know what Brunner will do to

you if he gets his hands on you after you squealed? He'll break your neck with his two hands."

Lippel looked very sick.

"I think you'd better come with me, just for your own protection."

"What you going to do with me?"

"Am I going to turn you over to the law? I might. I might not. I haven't decided. I suppose it depends on you. I'm not the ungrateful kind. You help me and I'll help you."

"Please don't let Brunner know. I'll do anything you say, only let on I'm gone, let on I skipped the country."

"Get your mackinaw," Tim said without trying to hide his contempt.

The men were still shouting to Lippel, but none of them suspected what was going on. Lippel got his things together and said, "O.K., let's go."

They left by the back door. The door would not close. It's hinges had been sprung free of the wall.

The men were at the front door now and one of them started beating on the door, shouting, "Hey, open up! We're all out of coal oil."

"Just walk," Tim said to him, and they followed his tracks away from the building.

Tim expected to be seen and challenged and he planned what he would do, but the toughs remained on the other side of the cabin, talking in low voices among themselves, planning some new way of be-deviling Lippel.

"You don't know what I put up with," Lippel whined.

"Yes. There's an old fence here. Be careful." He didn't want to carry him with a broken leg. "I'll let no harm come to you. You're too valuable."

On the other side of the buried fence, with its drift hiding them, Tim said, "Coal oil? Did they say coal oil?"

"Yes."

"Where is it?"

"I got a can in the far corner. It's my oil, too, bought it with my own money, hired an Injun to haul it all the way here from Vermilion on a toboggan. They burned up all theirs and all I had, too, and now this that I bought with my own money—"

"Wait for me."

He did not know whether Lippel would wait or not. He ceased to care much. He had learned what he had come to learn. He felt to make sure of his matches in the watertight can in his pocket. The men were still on the far side of the house. For the time being they had given up on Lippel.

He went inside, found the coal oil, about two gallons in a five-gallon can, and poured approximately half of it around on the floor and on the base logs. He set it afire. He hurried outside and climbed the knoll to the rear of the lean-to.

He intended to apply the remainder of his kerosene to the lean-to, but its thick banking of earth and snow made it futile.

They had just noticed the fire in the cabin and were shouting to Lippel. Someone was trying to kick the door in. They had not yet discovered the back door open and Lippel gone.

He went down a steep pitch and reached the front of the lean-to. Horse blankets had been used as doors across its entrances. He lifted one of the blankets and went inside. It was dark. The place smelled of earth, pine needles, and sweaty clothes.

"Hello!" he said. "Is anyone here?"

He got no answer. He lit a match. Log-frame bunks filled with pine and spruce boughs were built along one side, but no one was there. He walked the length of the lean-to pouring kerosene all over the walls, bunks, and floor. He lit it and went outside.

By this time the cabin was an inferno, and they found that Lippel was gone. It was still fifteen or twenty seconds before anyone noticed that the lean-to was also on fire.

The guards came running from the railroad shouting to ask what the trouble was. "That dirty bastard, Lippel!" a man called back. "He burned us out."

The flames were now very bright, bursting through the roofs. Tim Chipman walked down the path, making no show of escape, and no one noticed him. He doubled back along the buried fence and found that Lippel was gone. He never expected to see him again, but in the timber near the cabin line the man called to him.

"Tim?"

"Yes."

"Alone?"

"Yes."

"Well," Lippel chortled, "we sure as the devil gave 'em their kerosene, didn't we?"

Tim did not take time to gloat with him. He ran back along the tracks to the log yard. The engine was there with steam up, having just hauled down a load of logs from Chilkao.

"Don't bother to unload," he called as he ran alongside. "That will be our first cargo to Mad River. We're going through tonight."

A whoop went up from men who had grown impatient from delay. One of the most vocally warlike was Ax-Handle Ole. He located a pint of moose milk in Lippel's war sack, downed it at one long tilt, threw the empty bottle far out into the forest, and now went stamping up and down the track, waving an ax handle, bellowing:

"Bane Ax-Handle Ole. Bane toughest fightin' man in nort' woods. You feller stay har. I go down thar all alone and clean out the yoint."

Johnson got in front of Ole and asked, "What if you run into Brunner down there?"

Ole was quite certain that Brunner would not be there. "Ain't afraid of no Brunner. I yust hope he is there, by golly. He won't get chance to yoomp on me from behind tonight."

But Ole did not go down to clean out the yoint all alone after all. Instead he stamped and sang his way back up the track for another look inside Lippel's war sack, but the liquor was gone.

Tim found a couple of rifles, which he placed in the engine cab. Half a dozen men wanted to ride up front. He chose Mahon and Johnson. Mahon was quite young and Johnson had a crazy way about him, but still he considered them the coolest heads among the volunteers.

Standing by the engine, Tim shouted back through cupped hands, "You boys hired out to be timberjacks. That's good enough for me. I'm not asking anybody to get shot for my outfit. If bullets start flying around, I want you to stay under cover. As far as that goes, there'll be no hard feelings if somebody wants to get off the train right now."

He meant it, but it made him feel good when nobody took him up on it. He mounted to the cab beside Mahon and Johnson. It was a downgrade, so all he had to do was release the break and budge the throttle to get the train rolling. They moved from the log yard into the timber. The timber was a solid black wall on both sides. When snow blocked them he had to use power, driving the engine's snowplow front, and when it became too deep for that, he stopped, summoned help, and waited to be shoveled out. In half an hour they came up to the barricade.

Tim stopped there, got down, and walked ahead with his rifle. He could see the shape of the barricade in front of him, the black growth of timber beyond, and a slight reddish light marking the location of the burned-out cabin and lean-to.

He called, "Hello in there!"

No one answered, but there was a movement, something he could feel rather than hear, and he knew that men were watching him.

"This is Tim Chipman," he said. "I have Lippel with me." That was a lie; he had left Lippel behind. "He's sold out to me. This is my property now, boys. You keep me off and you'll end up in the gow. You try to rough us up and you'll end up so deep in the gow it'll take a C.P.A. to find you. So think it over."

"Stay back!" The voice from the near darkness surprised him. It was Dick Poole's.

"Dick?"

"Yeah."

"We're coming through, Dick."

"You try it and you'll get lead in your guts."

Dick's presence there made it worse. Dick wasn't just trying to make an easy buck, like the other boys; he had a score to settle.

Tim walked to the barricade. The timber shadow was behind him and he was quite sure they could not see him, but still he felt like a man spotlighted on a stage.

He carried the Winchester in both hands. He laid it across the barricade. He did everything slowly. He could hear the noises of the engine behind him, and movements of men in the brush ahead. The barricade was a cribwork of logs, none of the logs thicker through than his legs. He lifted one of them, swung it around, and tossed it aside. It struck with a dull thud and came to rest in a snowdrift. A gun exploded, its flame making a white flash and streak in the timber. The bullet, glancing, made a ping and whine, but not close, somewhere along the grade ahead.

"Stay away!" Poole shouted.

He should have planned his attack better. Mahon, back in the engine, called his name. Then a gun exploded from the cab and he heard the whip of a high-velocity bullet seven or eight feet above his head.

"Hold your fire!" he shouted, but it was too late. Nobody could hear him.

Rifles went whanging back and forth between the woods and the engine.

While they were shooting, Tim moved more of the logs and succeeded in getting through the barricade. Now he was on the claim side with nothing to protect him. He went crabwise, feet first, down the grade. It wasn't a high grade. It had been dug in a hurry; it consisted of little more than two ditches with the dirt tossed over to form a ridge where the rails were laid.

He crawled along the ditch closer to Poole and his men, using its face for protection. Here and there water had accumulated, a cold slush. He kept going. He wanted to get on the far side of them. Nothing could make them feel worse than to be burned out and have guns on the wrong side.

He stopped, realizing that to go farther he would have to expose himself on the path that led up to the burned-out cabin. They were very close. He could hear their movements, apparently right at his elbow, but the shooting had stopped; the last shot had been fired half a minute ago. A raw odor of powder still hung on the air.

He decided to surprise them. "Put your guns down, boys."

There were sharp movements of surprise. "Yah!" a man said, and he heard the thud of a gun being dropped.

"Walk toward the house," he said.

It was ridiculous, he could not see them any more than they could see him, but he knew how they felt—exactly the same way that he had felt a few minutes before on the other side of the barricade.

Poole was shouting at his men, cursing them. One of them shouted back, "Go to hell! I'm not layin' down my life for Brunner—man that won't even spot you a jug of whisky. I'm gettin' out of here."

They wrangled back and forth, all the while retreating little by little through the timber. Then he heard Ax-Handle Ole charging through the undergrowth.

"Har, noo!" Ole bellowed. "You coom har and fight like a man, Poole. You har me, Poole? You dirty fink, coom out har and fight."

But nobody stopped to fight. They stopped arguing, and the forest swallowed them. The engine moved through the barricade. More men came down from Chilkao and fell to work with shovels, clearing the track. At dawn the first logs arrived at the brink of Mad River Canyon.

Ax-Handle Ole, still talking fight, stood shaking his fist and his ax handle in the direction of Talka. "Brunner, we beat you this time!" he shouted.

Tim said, "Yeah, but the lad may have a rifle or two left in him yet."

It was like Steve had said; the only time some men are licked is when they're dead.

Chapter Seventeen

Down at Talka, Lynne Tilton noticed when the strange men arrived, and she wondered about it. They did not have the appearance of timberjacks or mill hands, and it was not the time of year when much new labor was put on. She would have asked Brunner about them, but he was not yet back from Prince Albert.

Lynne was at her desk in the office, working on a map of the company holdings, when Dick Poole came in.

A bandage of gauze and adhesive tape covered almost half of his face, giving him a lopsided look. He remarked that he had heard a speeder come up from Vermilion, and he wanted to know whether Brunner was on it. Lynne told him, "No."

When he turned to the door, she stopped him by asking, "What happened to your face?"

He answered truculently, "Piece of wood hit me. Inch more and it'd have got my eye."

"Snag?"

"No."

His surly tone angered her, and it occurred to her that there was some association between his face and those rough-looking men who had arrived.

"Where did those men come from? Were they up at Lippel's?"

He nodded.

"Did you get into a fight with the Chipman bunch?"

He called Chipman a name, not a suitable one to his way of thinking, but as close to it as he dared in the hearing of a lady.

"What happened?"

"Sneaked in, burned us out, both cabins. Then when we came out they opened up on us with guns."

It wasn't the truth, and though Dick was a good enough liar, it did not sound like the truth. She did not like him. She knew he had been a spy at the Chipman camp, and she did not like spies. She did not see why Brunner always thought he had to have men like Dick Poole around.

She said, "I'd better phone and get the police out here."

131

"You better wait."

"Why?"

"Well, Brunner might not like it."

"You think the mountie might get at the truth."

"I told you the truth!"

"Who started the shooting?"

He shrugged and would have gone outside, but she had moved between him and the door.

"Where's Lippel?"

"Well may you ask, that yellow—" He couldn't name Lippel suitably, either. "Skipped out. Went over to 'em. He's the one that set the place afire, like to killed us all. I'd like to get my hands—"

"His name isn't really Lippel."

"Oh, yes, it is."

"He's not the original Lippel." It was a stab in the dark and she watched his face.

"I didn't know you knew that. But you do, so you can see why I wouldn't want to get the mountie up here, not without Brunner said O.K."

At the moment Lynne was talking to Dick Poole, Croft Brunner's ski-equipped plane was setting down to a dangerous landing on the ice and snow that ringed Chilkoos Lake. Ten minutes later he was on a speeder, being carried up the grade to Talka. There, about an hour later, he was met by Dick Poole, who told him what had happened at the Lippel claim the night before.

The news put Brunner in a shaggy-wolf humor. He walked on to the office, tramping in without bothering to wipe the mud off his boots. He stopped when he saw Lynne facing him.

Even in his present temper he had to stop and look at her. She was dressed in plaid—a plaid flannel shirt, a matching plaid skirt boxed off at the knees, a pair of Scotch tartan stockings, and high leather boots. Her hair was pulled back and knotted. Brunner forgot about the Lippel fracas for a few seconds while he looked at her. He generally observed every little unusual thing, but today he was so busy looking at her that he did not notice her mackinaw hanging on the tree by her desk, and the peculiar weighted sag to its right side where she had placed her .32 caliber revolver.

"Hello, Lynne," he said, and she answered pleasantly enough, but made no move to come toward him.

Things had changed, and he knew it. Brunner had been aware of the change for several months; in fact, ever since Tim Chipman had returned, the autumn before. The thought made him tighten up inside. He wanted her, he was in love with her. He considered her a fit mate for him. He often thought, What kids we could raise!

"Did he tell you about it?" she asked.

"Who? About what?"

"Poole."

"Yes." He laughed, treating it lightly. "Lynne, come here. What kind of a welcome is this?"

She did not move. Something more than usual was troubling her.

She said, "He's sold out to Tim Chipman."

"What the devil are you talking about?"

"About Lippel, of course. He sold his claim to Chipman."

He shrugged his shoulders. "You're taking this too seriously, Lynne."

"Of course. The claim didn't even belong to him."

"Who the devil has been talking to you?" Tim Chipman, he thought, and it made him go hot and cold. To hide his feelings he walked to the basin, poured water, and washed his hands. At last he was able to say in a careless voice, "Whoever it was told you that, he was wrong. He's Lippel, as our lawyers have charged us a pretty penny to prove, and as Chipman's lawyers proved, too, much as they hated it."

"No. He's not the Lippel who took out the claim."

"Who told you?"

"What difference does it make?"

He looked at his big, blunt fingers to see if they were clean. He thought, I'd kill her with these hands before I'd let her go to Tim Chipman. He wondered what had passed between them, down in Vancouver, maybe, or here, while he was gone. He had an imagination that did him no good.

"Sure," he said. "What difference does it make?" He walked over. "To hell with Lippel. It's nothing for you to worry about. It's my affair. I'll take the blame for it."

"You acted for the partnership."

"So?"

"I'm pulling out."

He changed color. His complexion, under his tan, was grayish.

"You mean you're dissolving our partnership?"

"Yes."

In this same room, he was thinking, me and her dad! And now, here it was again. He pointed to the desk, her desk, which used to be her father's, at the maps and all the old ledgers of the Swiftwater Company.

"You've had time to go through them. Maybe you haven't. If not, you should. You ought to total up your indebtedness. Figure it up, what you owe. Not to me, to the others. Don't worry about what you owe me. I'll give you time on that. Just figure the rest. And make a guess how long you'd last, out on your own."

"I'll get by somehow."

She started as if to go around him, and he shifted his position to block her way.

"No, Lynne."

"I'm leaving."

"No. Not until—"

"Get out of my way!"

He laughed at her. It pleased him to see her so small and defiant. He admired her nerve. Yes, he thought, she's the woman for me. What kids we could raise!

He came toward her and she backed away. She thought of the revolver she had dropped in her mackinaw pocket. It was within reach, but if her hand went directly to the pocket he would know, and he would be able to spring forward and stop her. She would have to be more subtle. She took the mackinaw from its hook and slipped it on, and he did not try to stop her. Then she let her hands fall to the pockets as if by habit. She lifted the gun before he realized what she was doing, and she pointed it and rocked the hammer back.

He stopped. It took him a second to realize that she had the drop on him. He laughed. There was admiration in the sound. He said, "Girl, girl! What a girl you are!"

"I'll shoot!"

"No, Lynne. You won't shoot."

"Stay back."

"You're running a bluff. A good bluff, but you wouldn't kill a man. Now, give me the gun."

She cried with her voice on edge, "Croft, I will! I'll shoot!"

He kept coming. There was no place she could retreat to. Her hand clenched the gun very hard.

She fired. The gun came to life with a streak of flame in the dim room. Its explosion was shattering after the tense, quiet voices.

The gun was pointed chest-high. The bullet hit Brunner from a distance of only seven or eight feet. It knocked him off balance. He tried to come on and keep her from getting away, but he hit the corner of the desk. He almost fell. He saved himself by holding to the desk. Lynne was away from the wall, backing, facing him, the gun still pointed, not once taking her frightened eyes off him.

Brunner held to the desk for five or six seconds, recovering from bullet shock. It was only a .32 and it had not hit him in a vital spot, but still the shock of it kept his mind from focusing. He groped inside his shirt and brought a hand out covered with blood. He looked at his hand and looked around, and finally he shook the fog from his brain and started after her.

"Don't try to follow me!" she cried, her back to the door.

He laughed with a crazy sound. "That popgun!" he said. "Lynne, get yourself a gun, a real gun. Get a thirty-eight. You'll need that to stop me."

A man came running from outside, a truck driver named Seers. He burst in without knocking and stopped when he saw the gun, and saw Brunner with blood all over his hand.

"Hey, you're shot!"

"Keep away from me!" When he didn't move, Brunner shouted, "Get out! You dirty, meddling bastard, get out!"

Seers said, "O.K., O.K.!" and backed through the door, his eyes shifting from Brunner to Lynne.

Brunner called after him, "Find the Chink, tell him to get down here. And keep your mouth shut about this. It was only an accident."

Brunner sat down. He kept one hand pressed to his side while blood oozed through his shirt and between his fingers. He watched Lynne, who, still at the door, had put the gun back in her mackinaw pocket.

"Can I help you?" she asked.

He laughed bitterly. "What if I said yes? What could you do without getting close enough so I could get my paws on you? No, get out of here. Get out. Go up to him, why don't you? Go up to Chipman. He's the one you want, not me. And after all I did for you!"

She left, went home, and locked the doors, but he did not bother her. She did not come out until next morning, when, the gun still in her pocket, she went to the mill and hunted out a couple of her father's old-time employees and had them load some of her things on a handcar and speeder. Brunner did not stop her, even when she sent them to get the Swiftwater Company books from the office.

She glimpsed Brunner only once, striding from one of the sheds to the mill in his usual strong-legged, bull-moose manner. If the wound bothered him, he did not show it.

The speeder took her away. At Vermilion she had her things switched to the rusty old Swiftwater siding and unloaded at the long-closed bolt mill.

"You opening up here again?" one of the men asked, probably as a joke, for he looked surprised when she answered:

"Yes!"

Chapter Eighteen

At that moment in Chipman work was booming along as never before.

Only a few men were now engaged in getting out timber; almost all of them were down from the woods to work the jammers at Chilkao siding, or they were at the canyon to unload the steadily laboring train and swing the logs by means of high tackle over the edge and down to the river ice far below.

The weather had been warm. Pools of water had formed on the surface of the ice, and it became spongy near the shores. The south sides of the hills were bare and streams were running in many of the gulches, tunneling under the snow.

Tim Chipman had hoped for a late breakup. He cursed the warm weather. Without additional tackle, logs commenced to stack up at the canyon. He stripped his Nokewin Lake camp for equipment, using most of it for repairs. He was desperate for cable, the heavy cable needed to handle those huge Chilkao logs, but there was none available closer than Prince Albert.

Lack of cable finally brought the canyon work to a standstill. In desperation he was about to construct rollways when John Ellis, a trapper who once had been a river hog on the Swiftwater payroll, came up with news that Lynne was in Vermilion with four men fixing the old mill, and that she had a quantity of wire rope for sale.

"How's my credit?" Tim asked, and laughed, making it sound like more of a joke than it was.

"It must be good. She already got the stuff out and loaded."

"How?" He was thinking of the dismantled railroad.

"Team and sled."

There had been rumors about some shooting in Talka and about her departure, but there were always rumors and three fourths of them were lies. He had not dared even believe it before. Now Ellis' news made him feel good all over.

Still, she would have some trouble getting that wire rope past Brunner.

He kept thinking about it. He was unable to sleep
more than a couple of hours that night. He got up at
dawn, made himself a wolf pack, and walked to Vermilion.

He found one man at the old bolt mill. He stopped
working on a compressor, wiped grease off his hands on a
piece of waste, and said yes, the wire rope was gone,
Lynne herself and a couple of the boys had started
out with it the day before. They had a four-horse
team and sled, and they were planning on breaking
through by the old road on the Mad River side.

Tim stopped long enough for grub, then set out to
follow the sled tracks. They were easy to follow. Darkness
settled, and he went on by moonlight. The wire rope
was evidently quite a load, and it gave them plenty of
trouble in the deep, wet snow. He kept seeing Lynne's
small boot tracks and the tracks of the two men. Then
he found a great many tracks, and soon after the sled
changed directions, turning toward Talka. So the thing
had happened. Brunner had stopped the cable from
going through.

He forgot his fatigue and ran. The tracks were fresh,
perhaps only a couple of hours old. After a mile he
glimpsed firelight through the trees.

He had carried his revolver quite steadily since that
affair at Lippel's claim, and now he drew it. He expected
them to have a sentry out, but he walked up to the little
clearing and looked around at the scene lit by the fire
without being challenged.

There was no sentry. They felt that safe. The sled
had been unhitched and the horses were being fed
from the box. Men were sprawled around the fire,
some on new-cut spruce boughs, others on folded
mackinaws. A pot of coffee sat at the edge of the fire.
He recognized some of them to be the men he had
driven off Lippel's claim; others were strangers. He
counted seven, but there might be more on the far
side of the sled.

He walked on quietly into the firelight. One man
looked up. He saw who it was and sat popeyed, looking
at the gun.

Tim spoke. "Don't move, boys."

His voice startled the camp, but no one went for a
gun.

A man got to his feet. "Tim!" he said. The man was Dick Poole.

Tim laughed, showing his contempt, and said, "Well, Dick, so now they got you out fighting the women. What a hell of a job for a logging man!"

Dick cried, "This is Brunner's cable, and his road, too, if you'll look around. You're trespassing."

"Where is she?"

"Who?" Dick tried to stall, hoping one of his boys would have guts enough to sneak around through the bushes and get the drop. But at that moment, Lynne stood up behind the sled.

"Here I am."

Poole, very surly, muttered, "We weren't keeping her prisoner, so wipe that sneer off your face. We made her stay till daylight for her own protection."

They were holding her, Tim knew, until Brunner arrived, and it would have been up to him.

He said, "You'd better come along."

She was getting her things together. "Where's my gun?" she asked.

Someone handed her a rifle. She worked the lever far enough to make certain there was a loaded cartridge in the barrel. Then she smiled at Tim and said, "Now I can be of some help."

There were a couple of men getting ready to leave with her. Tim recognized one of them to be Shipley, who had worked for Swiftwater Tilton as a sawyer twenty years before.

They exchanged greetings and Shipley said, "How about this wire rope? Don't you need it?"

"I'm desperate for it, but we're out of luck. We could never get it through. It would take four days along these snowed-in trails, and with all the bushwhackers Brunner could scrape up—"

Lynne cried, "It's my cable! If I—"

"Listen, kid, with you helping me I'll carry those logs down the canyon in my arms."

He really felt like that. It was something to have her with him. He felt unbeatable. He did not give a damn for Brunner and all the rough-toughs that Brunner could find north of the border. He almost wished Dick Poole *would* start some trouble, but Dick remained where he was, leaning against the box of the sled, chewing tobacco, mean and watchful, but without the willingness to make a gamble.

They headed toward the ridge, taking turns at breaking trail through the soft, wet snow. It was slow going. Darkness led to false trails, and they had to turn back. At last they found a dog-sled trail on the summit. They rested in a jack-pole lean-to, and went on through early daylight and through the warm morning sun.

They heard the tackle creaking for a mile before they reached camp; somehow they had patched it up and got it working again.

"How in hell'd you do it?" Tim asked Lars.

"Stuck it together with good old babiche leather. You don't believe that, hah? What the hell, we got to get logs down. River about ready to bust loose. Ice starting to creep. Yust a little, but she's goin'."

Tim, who had an hour's nap in the lean-to, was in better shape than Lars, who had been almost forty-eight hours with no sleep at all. He talked in his slow manner, his eyes glazed, looking at Tim and at Lynne without seeing anything in the least surprising about her being there.

Tim asked, "How much has it moved?"

"Oh, I don't know, little here, little there. You can hear those damn logs go boom-boom all night. Ol' ice she growls, too. But she'll hold out for two-three day yet, maybe week."

Lynne said, "Just so it breaks big," and Lars wagged his head and said, "Yah."

The Mad was good for that one big surge, and they would be all right if the logs caught it and were carried down on its crest without a jam, but if they jammed and the flood was lost they would have to wait for next year, or, if they got deadheaded or rolled up against the shore reefs, they might have to wait forever.

Tim sent the girl to his shanty to get some sleep. He felt pretty fair now that the logs were moving again, but an hour later the tackle broke again, and this time when they mended it, it got hung up in the big bull block high above, and there it was despite all attempts to free it.

They worked through the day, men high aloft on the spar tree, men pull-hauling the cable from the ground. The splice was cut and the cable fell like a ton of snake. They worked through the night. Now, in the quiet, the deep booming of ice could be heard, although below, in the canyon depths reached by moonlight, scarcely any ice was visible; it was submerged by logs. Here and there water gushed, making streams and fountains from the deep current. In a couple of places the logs had moved sufficiently to become jammed, and some of the big sticks upended, thrust up like thick, truncated masts, but as yet it was not serious.

A Beaver Indian arrived from the back country pulling a toboggan loaded with pelts, and reported that the upper Mad had already broken up, but that the float ice had jammed and held the stream back, and already a mile-long stretch of lake had formed.

Steve Riika suggested they wait no longer, but go upstream and blast the ice dam to start their drive on that surge of water, but Tim said no; setting such a blast would be too great a risk for the men whose jobs it would be to carry and set the powder, and besides, the dam might hold for days or weeks, giving them an even larger initial flood.

Next morning there was fresh excitement: Old Cappy, the cook from Chipman, got there ready to collapse from running and reported that Brunner and a gang of men were on their way with dynamite to "blow hell out of things."

Questioned, Cappy could only repeat that they were going to "blow hell out of things." He was overweight from his own cooking, and from the wine he made of molasses and dried figs, and now he collapsed on a bench beside the cook shack and said, "Kid hear 'em. He's got a little bobtailed trap line. They're hauling dynamite. Wagonloads. Ton of it. Bring me liquor. I'll die if I don't get liquor and black coffee. Dynamite. They're going to blow hell out of things."

"It's a little late for him to be blowing hell out of things," Tim said, looking ruefully at his broken tackle.

Cappy's news took on importance when Johnson came down from the spar tree and asked what was going on down at the Narrows. Men were there, half a dozen anyway, and they were at work among the great pillars of basalt that towered over that particularly narrow and vertical portion of the canyon.

Tim hurried aloft, getting above the smaller trees, getting a view of the canyon below.

The canyon was not a single precipitous drop. It was cracked and columnar. In places it was a broad U, again it resembled a series of ragged cracks in the earth, as though it had been pulled roughly apart. At the Narrows, about four hundred yards downstream, the basaltic walls were broken by pillars and irregular masses, all cubed out by weathering and the natural jointing of that type of rock, standing rather precariously, block on block, ready to collapse if just one certain block were ever removed. In places one could see where older masses and towers had collapsed, and these, slumping across the canyon, had been somewhat washed away and eroded, but enough remained to form rapids, a peril to canoe travel. If some of the other masses went down, they might easily form an obstacle to his log drive; they might even stack it up into a disastrous jam that would cause him to lose the flood and ruin him altogether.

He saw no one at the Narrows, but he could see the trail they had followed, a muddy strip through snow, and he waited no longer.

Descending, he was met by Johnson, who had just heard what Cappy had to say.

"We better stop those bastards or they'll blow the whole damn wall in!"

Johnson ran inside the shack and popped out again, rangy and long-legged, happy at the prospect of violence, dragging a Winchester.

"Hold it!" Tim said. "Rush into this and get your head shot off. You can't do it alone. Get Lars and Mahon. And Marr. Marr's been spoiling for a fight. And Ole, he's a fighting man. I've still got lumps on my head from that fellow."

Men commenced gathering around as news of trouble spread through camp and down the track toward Chilkao. Ax-Handle Ole came with the others, not eagerly, but hanging back and apprehensive.

Marr saw him and jeered, "What's wrong, Ole? Losing your guts?"

"No, by golly," Ole said, hunching his shoulders and swinging his massive head back and forth. "Got plenty guts. Bane fightin' man. But I don't fight wit' guns. I whip whole damn saloonful of Irishmen wit' ax handle, but guns—"

"Lay off him," Tim said. "I'm not asking anyone to duck bullet lead."

There were more willing to go than there were guns to equip them. Tim started away with nine men follow-ing. When he got them together down the trail, he made a little talk, saying he wanted no shooting if he could help it; a show of force would probably be enough here, just as it had been on Lippel's claim. Nobody believed that, however. He did not even believe it himself, because it was getting toward the showdown, and Brunner was not the man to be whipped.

They walked on, quietly, apprehensively. It became so quiet that their footsteps on the trail seemed loud.

A hundred yards downstream from the spar tree it, started. A rifle whanged with a high-velocity impact, and its bullet snapped through spruce branches overhead.

It was not aimed to kill. It was a warning. Close enough to make a man go for the ground, but still a warning.

All except three or four had found cover. Tim told them to get out of sight. He stayed out of sight himself. He moved on a few steps in the cover of trees. The shot had come from a little knoll across a clearing about three hundred yards away.

The young timber topper Maguire had followed him. When Tim stopped, Maguire plodded straight ahead, his eyes on the knoll.

"Come back!" Tim called to him.

Maguire did not seem to hear him. He kept right on going through scrubby trees, into the open. The gun cracked again. Its bullet was low this time, almost at the toes of Maguire's boots, digging a furrow through wet snow, making a black furrow as it mixed dirt with the snow. And the gun whanged again, not intended to warn this time, but aimed at Maguire's knees.

Maguire was running now. A haze of powder smoke marked the gun's position among rocks and low growth, and Tim fired at it. Other men, coming up behind him, opened fire. There were six or seven shots singing as the bullets glanced from rocks here and there on the knoll, momentarily diverting attention from Maguire. Then guns answered from other points on the knoll.

Maguire went down. He seemed to have tripped. He got up and ran, but bent far forward, arms almost dangling to the snow, the rifle actually dragging. He fell again. It was obvious now that he had been hit. He crawled through foot-deep snow on hands and knees and lay on his face behind a deadfall log.

"Stay down!" Tim shouted over and over through cupped hands. "We'll have to get him," he said.

Marr was heading into the open. "The dirty bush-whackers! I'm going up there—"

Tim dragged him back. When Marr tried to jerk away, Tim almost flung him off his feet.

"We'll get him, but be cool about it." He motioned to Steve Riika. "You take command here. Don't let 'em go off half-cocked. Circle around on the downstream side. That's where they don't want us. Make that ridge —it overlooks the canyon."

"How about Maguire?" Marr asked.

"I'll get him."

He went by himself at a trot, keeping in the trees. He could no longer see Maguire, but he could see the root end of the deadfall like the claws of a bird reaching four or five feet from the snow. The timber played out. He got down and crawled. He was now in the clearing. He found the cover of an old stump. After that he was protected by a low tangle of wiry buckbrush. Moving swiftly on hands and knees or on his belly, he got halfway across the clearing without being spotted.

Before him lay a smooth bulge of ground without the slightest concealment. He rose to a sprinter's crouch, took a sight on his goal, and sprinted.

Guns pounded. He felt the whip of lead. Then the log was in front of him. He saw Maguire turned, looking at him, then he dived headlong and was safe.

Maguire was still staring at him.

"How are you?" Tim asked.

Maguire managed to talk, slowly, thick of tongue. "Hell, boss, I'm O.K. Just a burn."

"Get down farther."

"No, I'm all right. They're not going to shoot at me and get away with it. I'll—"

Tim had to pull him to the ground and wrestle with him. Maguire finally lay on his back while Tim sat on him. Still sitting on him for fear he would make a sudden leap to his feet, Tim had a look at his wound. There was blood making his wool-blanket trousers heavy in the region of his right hip. He got the pants down and the underwear away so he could look at it. It was such a bloody mess he couldn't tell; but probably it looked worse than it was, because the blood did not come in spurts, and apparently he had been hit in no vital spot.

"You're all right," he said to reassure him.

"Sure I'm all right. All I need is a chew of tobacco."

"I've got some."

Maguire stuffed his mouth with the strong tobacco, grinned, and said, "Bullet can't hurt a man that can chew this stuff."

Tim had no bandage, only a dirty handkerchief. He could not move Maguire under the muzzles of those rifles. He had only one course—to drive them off the knoll.

He put his mackinaw around Maguire and told him to wait.

"I'm comin'!" Maguire said.

"I still give the orders. You stay!"

He went around the butt end of the log, crawling through snow. With the log behind, a drift still hid him. He looked back and saw Maguire a couple of yards behind.

"You're fired!" Tim said.

"You sonuvabitch," Maguire said, grunting with each word, "I wouldn't have got paid anyhow."

"Anyway, keep the muzzle of that rifle up. Fill it with snow and it'll backfire your head off."

"O.K."

They kept going, in the open now, without drawing a shot. They reached some brush. Tim watched, gun ready, tense for movement on the knoll, which was now just beyond and above.

A man was running, far off; they caught the thudding, drumlike weight of him through the snow, but no one was in sight.

They kept going. The knoll was cross-tracked this way and that. Here was a log where a man had been lying, and here some empty cartridges lay in the snow. The knoll was abandoned.

Maguire said, "What the hell, now?" and sat down. He was pale. He had lost blood and his right leg was growing stiff. Tim half led him, half carried him back to the camp and set out to find the group under Riika.

He was running along the canyon rim, almost at the place where the gunfire had started, when the earth rocked under him and concussion almost knocked him down.

Wind whistled in the trees. Stones ripped the branches high above. The blast was followed by a thunder of falling rock.

"Get down, get down!" he could hear Riika shouting somewhere ahead.

He ran again. He found a spot from which the canyon was visible. A cloud of dust hung over the Narrows, filling the canyon from wall to wall. The dust billowed and opened, giving him a brief view. One of the great pillars of basalt was falling. He saw it slump across the ice, carrying lesser pillars before it. The backfire of the explosion loosened another mass against the wall. It hung for a second and slumped, burying the lesser slide beneath it. Then the dust came thicker than ever, hiding all from his view.

Chapter Nineteen

B<small>RUNNER'S</small> <small>MEN</small> had disappeared. Their work was done; a mass of rock dammed the canyon.

Tim returned to camp. The boys had armed themselves with anything they could find—clubs, axes, peaveys, hooks, and one of Halseth's Swedes was carrying an improvised bomb, four sticks of dynamite in a baking-powder can.

They crowded around him and followed him as he walked, asking what he was going to do. He did not know himself.

He saw Halseth and said, "Take the engine and some of the boys over to the home camp and load on all the powder you can find. There's nineteen or twenty cases there, and half a dozen more at Chilkao. Bring them all."

Evening was almost there when the little engine chuffed back, pulling a flatcar with the powder stacked behind a protective cribbing of logs.

"Now we got it, what'll we do with it?" Mahon wanted to know.

Below, the logs had started to move. Ice and logs came to rest against the rock dam. The forward logs, pushed from behind, churned and upended. The jam mounted higher and higher. It was the thing Brunner had aimed for, and he had brought it about.

Lefty Johnson, an old hand at the river drives, was less downhearted than the rest. "Wait till we get a head of water behind her. I've seen a big jam, big as that, bigger, so solid you'd think it was Boulder Dam, and yet if you find the one log, the old key log, boom! One firecracker would break it loose. Only thing is to find the one log."

The river was on the rise. All night they could hear the creaking, booming sound of it. A man was sent upriver to prospect the possibility of bringing an early crest by blasting the ice dam, but he returned with the discouraging word that a rift had developed and the lake was slowly emptying. There came a minor crest next sundown. The river fell until midnight, then started to rise again. Water rose by degrees all the next day, forming a lake behind the dam at the Narrows, but the dam was not solid, the fallen boulders acted as a mighty strainer, holding the logs and float ice but allowing the bulk of the river to roar beneath.

Steadily the logs piled up, the jam shortened. They pushed themselves like a creeping wave until their front members actually overhung the crest of basalt. Just when the jam seemed solidified there would be a splinter and thunder, and it would sag forward another few feet, but it never quite broke free of the obstruction.

Halseth came from upriver, soaked to the waist, and said, "Ol' river ain't going any higher. I told you long time ago this Mad wasn't logger stream. This is flood water we got. This is only damn flood we're going to get."

Tim asked, "How long will the crest hold?"

"Two, maybe three days."

"You've seen plenty of log jams, Lars. Can we open this one?"

"Yah, sure." He stood rubbing his four-day whiskers. They made a bristly sound under his shoe-leather hand. "We got twenty-sax cases dynamite. That's plenty powder. With twenty-sax cases powder we could blow logs all the way to Beaver Lake, by golly."

When Tim asked for volunteers to carry powder down the treacherous goat trails to the log jam, almost every man in camp responded.

He chose thirteen of them; that would make it two trips for each. He then supervised their preparations. He had them make rope slings and tumplines, because dropping a case of 60-per-cent dynamite could lead to an unfortunate conclusion, especially when the dynamite had been frozen and thawed out as this had, making it, by common belief, as temperamental as a red-haired woman.

When things were completed to his satisfaction, with half a dozen detonating caps wrapped in a handkerchief and with a coil of fuse around his neck, Tim descended for the first look-around.

The trail at the brink of the canyon was muddy and treacherous. He went carefully, testing his way, thinking of the men who would come after him with loads on their backs. Over his arm he carried the .405 Winchester he had high-graded from the station house at

Vermilion. Vodal was above him with the longer-range
.270, watching for snipers, for it would be like Brunner
to anticipate trouble and try to prevent any blasting of
his dam.

Tim told himself that he was safe enough. Brunner
had placed himself too far on the bad side of the law
already; he would not take the further chance of com-
mitting murder. For example, they had not tried to
kill Maguire that day—they had fired low, at his legs.
Such thoughts, as he exposed himself, an excellent
target against the cliffs, made him feel better, but
not much.

The path took him along a rough eighty-degree wall
of basalt. It was an ancient portage trail that had been
traveled by the fur *voyageurs* as much as 150 years
before, and by Indians for a thousand years before
that. Here and there an accumulation of snow or wet
pine needles still made his footing precarious, but it
was better than the mud above. Should a man slip,
there were usually some wire-tough roots of juniper
or a projection of rock for him to grab hold of.

Thus he traveled, switchback, about fifty yards, and
was at a point about that many feet vertically below
the canyon edge. He was alone. His men were above,
hidden by trees, sitting around on their cases of powder,
waiting for him to give the signal from below. He stopped for a look below.

There were no shores to the river now. It had risen
too far for that. In fact, he could see no river, either.
No water, only the solid, jammed, floating mass of
logs, creaking as they moved this way and that, scrap-
ing the rock walls.

A bullet struck, powdering fragments of stone against
his cheek, stinging him, leaving a burned smell. He
instinctively flattened himself against the wall, but he
realized at the same moment that the shot had come
from far away, across the canyon, and that there was
no protection for him.

He ran down the trail. At a switchback he found
partial cover behind a lump of rock. He looked across,
trying to locate movement or the smoke of a gun. He
saw neither.

The man fired again, and almost at the same instant
he heard the closer crack of the .270 above.

Vodal had seen someone, but he had missed and was cursing because he had missed him.

Tim waited with the .405, a ponderous old gun, wondering how high he would have to aim if he was to arch its bullet over there and do any harm. But he still could not tell where the shots were coming from.

"There's two of 'em!" Vodal shouted.

Tim moved back along the path, back to the wall, watching for movement, hoping the threat of Vodal's .270 would keep them under cover, and it did.

Reaching concealment in the scrub timber, he said, "We'll have to wait for dark. They'd have us like ducks at a Vancouver shooting gallery."

Mahon remarked that he'd rather take chances on bullets than on that cliff trail after dark. "Get hit by a bullet, you might live through that. But how'd you like to fall a couple hundred feet to that jam? Come night and that canyon will be as black as a gambler's heart."

They wrangled over it, and most of the men were for tackling it right then, trusting to Vodal and a few more riflemen to keep these snipers occupied.

Then Tim said wait, he had a better idea, and walked along the canyon testing the wind. There was a down-draft. Fires above would put smoke into the canyon. In that way they would have light to travel by, and protection from Brunner's snipers at the same time.

He sent men to get the fires going, and waited. A good share of the first smoke rolled back over the forest, but slowly, very slowly, the canyon became filled with blue-white haze.

When the far wall was only a shape through the smoke with none of its smaller features discernible, Tim said, "All right, let's go."

He waited for them to get their loads right. He started with Steve Riika at his heels with a case of powder on his back and a peavey for a walking support. Others followed at intervals of twenty or thirty feet. The smoke was not solid, but hung in layers. Then the breeze quickened and the smoke blew in so heavily it blotted out the far wall of the canyon, and even the ice and the float logs below.

Few words were spoken. No one fired at them. Thirty feet above the water the smoke was limpid, thinly diffused. It seemed very quiet there, close to the river. A stone rattled with a click, click, click and thudded to rest among the logs. It was on the far side.

Tim stopped. He stood with his back to the cliff, braced with his boots set, his gun ready.

"Hi-ya!" called Vodal from above. He had tried to startle someone. The .270 whanged with a brittle clap-whack of explosion and echo.

A gun answered from the far side. Somewhere above, in the haze, a bullet pinged and glanced away.

Quiet again. Tim, through cupped hands, called to his men, "Just keep coming. Easy. They can't see us. The smoke is thickening."

"They came close enough to *me*," said a voice he recognized as Stimak's.

Guns came to life on both sides of the canyon in some blind shooting. "Save it up!" Tim shouted, fearing some wild bullet would explode one of the boxes of powder, but no one paid the slightest attention.

He moved on. The path descended slowly, a step here and there, its goal a ledge of rock, now submerged, from which the *voyageurs* launched their canoes.

At last he was able to step from the path to the log jam.

He chose a horizontal log, tested it with his hobs, and put his weight on it. The log might, from its solidity, have been set in concrete. He went on, testing his way. A quarter of the distance across he stopped and watched his men single-file along the path, much too close together, each carrying enough powder to blow him to Victoria.

Thirteen cases, he decided, would be enough. He did not want to push his luck too far.

"Where you want it?" Steve Riika asked.

"You're an old river hog. Where do *you* want it?"

"O.K., come along."

Steve took the lead; he walked with no more apparent care than if he had been on solid ground. An old-timer of the river-drive days, he had contempt for the industry's modern preference for trucks and trailers.

He climbed the apex of the jam. Here were logs pushed at every angle. Some, upended in groups, left holes through which one could look twenty feet down and see a swirling current from the river.

Riika climbed to the downstream side and back again without putting down his load of powder; he located a log, nodded, and shot a brown stream of snoose toward it.

"There's your key log, Tim. I'll bet you just fifteen-twenty sticks of powder put right, good and deep, will knock that log out and the whole damn thing will go. In the old days, let me tell you, we didn't even use powder. Old-time lumberjacks just used peavey and hook. We fought with peavey and hook, too, and good old hobnails, none of those coward guns."

Johnson was there with his powder, and after him Marr, and then Stimak. Smoke kept blowing in, thicker and thicker on the wind, but the same wind blew holes in the smoke through which, briefly, high areas of the side could be seen.

Tim did some figuring on the basis of thirteen cases of powder. He would put nine cases here, and put two against each shore to explode as secondary blasts and break up the drag.

Minutes had passed without gunfire. Now a rifle exploded. It was Vodal. A gun answered him. They kept firing across the canyon, blindly, at the sound of each other's guns through the haze.

The powder was all there now. Tim had it lowered by ropes, a case at a time, into a crevice near the key point. One of the last cases was broken open, a stick of powder was removed, capped, primed.

"How much?" Johnson asked with his jackknife ready to cut the fuse.

Tim measured nine feet and marked the point.

"Little close?" Lefty asked.

"Two feet to the minute, four and a half minutes, what the hell?"

Johnson cut the fuse and notched it. He had crimped the cap tight with his teeth; he tried it now to make sure the fuse would not pull loose. Then as an extra precaution he used a string to tie the fuse and cap tightly to the side of the stick. He put the primer back among the other sticks in the box and pressed the slat back in place. Carefully this most important part of the charge was lowered into place, and the last of the nine cases was placed atop it. The remaining cases were placed as deeply as possible among the logs at each shore, and these too were primed. The job had taken about fifteen minutes.

Some of the men were already up the side. Tim sent all except Johnson to follow them. Johnson, who took pride in being a powder man, insisted on remaining behind.

"Ready?" asked Johnson by the far shore.

Tim waited with matches and an unlit spitter fuse in his hands. He had intended to set all three charges himself, and had cut the fuses accordingly; now he wanted to wait about half a minute after the one by the far bank had been lit.

Johnson was on his hands and knees, trying to spit the fuse. Something had gone wrong. Only eight or ten seconds passed, but it seemed like a long time. Crouched and still, he could feel the steady rise and sink of the log mass. It was like a monster breathing. He got to thinking of the chance that one of these cases below might become pinched and ignited by pressure.

He saw the reddish burst of flame as Johnson got the fuse going. "O.K.," called Johnson, and he was up, hurrying with long steps across the logs.

Tim had his spitter going now. He was counting, forcing himself to count slowly, keeping track of the time. At twenty, Johnson was already out of sight through the smoke. He kept counting. A stone clattered down from the far side where Brunner's snipers were placed.

It could have fallen from far above, he told himself. But it had not come from above. He saw movement. A man was descending by means of a rope, holding the rope while digging his hobnails into the rough stone.

He had glimpsed the man through a wind-blown hole in the smoke. The smoke closed in again. He was to twenty-five on his count. When Brunner's voice came to his ears, through haze, it seemed only a foot away:

"Keep going, damn you, keep going!" Brunner was shouting at his man. "Keep going or I'll put a bullet through you!"

A second later the man let go of the rope, slid down the last few feet of canyon wall, and lit on one of the logs, balancing himself, a rifle thrust high overhead.

The man was Dick Poole.

He did not see Tim. He ran, dropped to partial concealment behind an upthrust log, and called, "All clear!"

Brunner answered, "Good! Wait and we'll cross together."

Tim lit the fuse. He wanted to do that before anything else. After that he would worry about Poole, about getting clear himself.

Then Poole saw him.

Surprise almost caused Poole to lose his balance. He caught himself with an outflung left arm. Lying half across a log, he got his rifle around. He fired, a snap shot, without aiming. The bullet whanged close, taking a chip from one of the logs at Tim's left.

Tim retreated. He had to save his spitter for the remaining charge. He did not worry about firing back at Poole so much as about getting the job done.

Brunner, unable to see through the smoke, was bellowing to Poole, asking what the trouble was, but Poole, now under cover, did not answer for fear of revealing his position.

"Dick, answer me! What did you run into?" Brunner called.

Tim retreated, backing away, watching for Poole and for Brunner. Something moved. It was in an unexpected direction. It was Poole. Poole saw him at the same instant. They both fired. Poole had been too hurried; he fired while turning, and Tim had frozen him against the .405's knife-edge front sight.

The heavy bullet of the old grizzly gun knocked Poole sprawling. He struck on his back across a log, the nail-studded bottoms of his boots the chief thing Tim Chipman could see. For an instant Tim thought he was dead. He was bullet-shocked. He turned himself over and lay across the log with arms and legs dangling; then slowly, groggily he crawled toward shore.

Tim could have killed him. He did not want to kill him. All he wanted was to get across to that third powder charge. He was being fired on from above. He paused to shoot back. The smoke had blown clear. He was in the open, a suicidal position.

A bullet stung him. He thought himself hit. It had ripped through the material of his mackinaw. As he pivoted, a piece of bark came loose under his boot, and he fell. He might have gone to his death among the logs. Instinctively he turned his rifle crosswise and got it under his body.

He cracked the stock just under the grip, but it saved him. He was there when Brunner came down the rope just as Poole had done a short while before. When Tim got his footing again, Brunner was nowhere to be seen.

Tim called, "You stay and get blown to hell if you want to, but we got thirteen cases of powder in here and the fuse is burning."

Brunner did not answer. A third man heard his voice and shot at him. The smoke, clearing as the draft became stiffer, placed Tim in the man's view. He was driven down again. He tried to retreat and still remain hidden. He did not know how much time had passed. He had stopped counting. He crawled, made it over the high forward hump of logs to the steep downstream end of the jam. He moved, clinging to log butts, crawling between them, among them. New-fallen rock and the raging river were below, and downstream it was white water as far as he could see.

His hobs slipped. He dropped his rifle to save himself. The rifle clattered twice and struck the water and disappeared.

He noticed the smoke had thickened again. He chanced going to the top. His own men, shooting from the canyon wall, helped him. He had dropped the spitter. He gave up all thought of setting that third charge. A minute and a half had passed. Just a guess, of course. He probably had three minutes left to get clear.

It seemed as though he had gone a long way from the main powder charge. He had not. He had doubled back on his course while saving himself. Now he was at the apex of the jam, and there was Brunner, lying full length on his stomach, an arm reaching far down, trying to grab the burning fuse.

Tim turned on him. Brunner did not realize he was there. He moved, driving his arm deeper and deeper. Then, at the last fraction of time, he saw him.

He had time only to roll on his back and grab his rifle to use as a club. Tim came boots first. He kicked the rifle aside and trampled it from his hands.

He tried to trample Brunner into the logs. Brunner saved himself by twisting over. He came to a crouch. He met Tim's charge, and they clinched.

Brunner stood. They traded lefts and rights. Toe to toe, they slugged it out for eight or ten seconds, neither willing to relinquish an inch, for to fall back would only give the other momentum.

Tim Chipman had the advantage of reach. He used a long left to keep Brunner off balance, trying to set him up for a right.

The left hand, landing repeatedly, mashed Brunner's lips. His mouth was filled with blood. He spat blood, but he was tough. He kept taking it.

Suddenly he bobbed low. He lunged, moving his pivot foot. His foot seemed to have gone from under him. He was almost on one knee. Chipman made a reflective movement to follow up. The advantage was not there. Brunner had not lost footing. He had excellent footing. He had turned; now he came back with a half pivot, swinging a right with all the solid power of his body, and Tim Chipman had walked into it.

It was the same blow that had felled Ax-Handle Ole. It was like being struck by a club. Tim went down.

He had had no sensation of being hit. He had scarcely seen the blow coming. He was just there, on the log, clinging through instinct.

His mind worked after a fashion. Everything—Brunner, his brain, his muscles—seemed to be slowed, barely moving. He said to himself, Brunner is coming to finish you under his hobs. Chipman, you have to get up. You have to do something. It was his mind talking to his body, and his body trying to act, and all in that frozen instant Brunner was on his way.

He got up to clinch. It was a mistake. Brunner kicked him in the head. He had a clean shot and kicked him brutally. Chipman went down. He was among the logs. He could feel their hard knocking against his body as he fell. He could feel a cold spray in his face. Everything was slick and wet around him. He hung, instinctively poking his elbows out, spreading his legs. A voice deep in the nerve cells of his brain shrieked that to go deeper would mean being swept away by the current, carried to death beneath the log jam. And there he hung in a nightmare of half awareness.

It might have been ten seconds, sixty seconds, an hour. He came up through waves of pain and light. He saw again. High above were triangles of light. He got hold of something, got his feet set on something. He climbed. He did not know how or where he climbed, only up, up, among logs, through a tiny opening. There was a log pushing him down. He had the terrible sensation of being trapped. He wriggled through, and suddenly he was free, able to stand.

Brunner stood in front of him. Brunner with his back turned, Brunner going down with his arm deep for one more try at the burning fuse.

Tim shouted something. He wanted Brunner to stand. He wanted him to stand so he could smash him down.

Brunner turned to his side. He saw him and got to his feet, retreating out of reach. Tim had momentum. He came straight on. He hit Brunner with a body block. He had put many an opposing hockey player into the boards with that one, and he had sat out many a penalty, but there was no referee to hamper him today.

He put Brunner down. Brunner got free and rose to his feet. He did it too quickly. He was unable to protect himself. Tim smashed him down. He tried to clinch. Tim rocked him loose with a left, and put him down again with a right.

Brunner fell among the logs. He crawled. "No," he said through battered lips. "No. Let's get — off here. Fuse—going. Wait. Stop. We'll both—blown to hell."

Tim stood and watched him crawl up the logs, crawl on hands and knees to the crest of the dam. He followed him. Tim was still groggy, unable to put things together in his mind, but he wanted to be close enough to put Brunner down whenever he tried to get up. Brunner did not try to get up. He got to the end of one log, fell from it, found another, and crawled along that.

Then explosion hit.

The force of it knocked Tim Chipman to his stomach. A log, rolling, threatened to crush him. He got to his feet. He ran without sense of direction, springing from log to log.

He thought groggily, I was right on top of it. How is it I'm still alive?

It came to his mind that he had cut the fuses wrong. It was not the big charge, but the small one set by

Johnson. So he was still alive. For a second or two he was still alive.

He was near the shore. He turned to look for Brunner. He was a fool, he knew it, stopping to look for him. Let him get blown to hell, it was what he deserved, but he had to stop and look. If he'd seen Brunner he'd have gone out for him. He didn't see him. He could see only the logs, the rocks and promontories of the far wall distorted in size and steepness by haze.

He heard a voice. It was Johnson. Where Johnson came from he never knew.

Johnson had hold of his arm. Urging him, cursing him, Johnson got him from the logs to the rock trail.

They ran together. Half blind from smoke and fatigue, Tim followed him on and on, climbing across talus rock, through tangled juniper, and there explosion hit again.

He knew enough to fall on his face. He pressed his face against the ground and wrapped his arms around his head. He was in a tiny gully. He felt himself sliding feet first through rock and juniper. He spread his legs stiffly until his boots dug in and stopped him.

Wood fragments rained and thudded. Whole logs boomed like thunder. Then there was another sound, deeper, a mountain-shaking roar, mounting.

"She goes, she goes!" Johnson was shouting.

He turned to look. The log jam had been blown apart. Briefly the blast had torn a depression to the river bottom. Then, as he watched, water, ice, and logs poured in and humped over the dam. The entire mass of logs was moving now. It parted the rock slide before it.

"You still alive?" shouted Johnson.

"Sure."

"By damn, there she goes! Whole damn winter's work. We're in business again, boy!"

They went on together. They took their time now. They rested every few steps to watch the movement of logs below. Tim kept thinking of Brunner. No man could have gone through that explosion and lived.

Something caught his eye. Something was moving among the logs. It was a man. The man was holding to one log, trying to pull himself toward shore with a free arm. A second man was on shore, following, a pole in his hands.

The man on shore was huge and plodding, like a bear walking on hind legs. Ax-Handle Ole.

Ole waded in shallow water, deeper and deeper, reaching out with the pole, but the man was afraid to let loose of the log for fear of slipping beneath, where there would be not a thousand-to-one chance of survival.

Finally he let go and seized the pole with both hands, and Ole maneuvered him through open water between two momentarily stranded logs.

There the man found bottom and walked. He staggered and got to shore, where he fell on his face. The man was Brunner. Somehow he had lived through it.

Ole bent and lifted him. He carried him in his arms. Tim thought he intended to take him like that higher up, to some dry spot under the cliffs. He did not walk toward the cliffs. He waded into the river. He lifted Brunner higher and higher.

Tim suddenly realized what he intended and shouted, "No, Ole, no!" but his voice was lost, and Ole would not have heeded anyway.

Brunner clawed furiously. He got hold of Ole's mackinaw. He saved himself for a second. Then, with a Gargantuan heave, Ole tore him loose and hurled him far out among the logs.

Brunner disappeared. Tim reached the canyon rim and ran along it, coming out each twenty-five or thirty yards from among the trees for another look at the river, but Brunner was gone. He was gone beneath the solid press of the log drive.

He stopped. He sat down. He was tired and a little sick. He went back to camp. His ears sang. The ground seemed to slant under him so it was hard not to walk in circles. Lynne had hold of him. She kept talking to him and he kept saying, "What? What?" She led him to the house. He sat down, shivering violently in his river-wet clothes. She put a tin cup in his hands. It was filled with a mixture of hot tea and whisky. He drank it and then he slept.

When he woke up it was night and he could hear the boys celebrating. Old Cappy, the cook, had brought up his molasses wine and they were just finishing it.

He asked about Brunner. Brunner was gone. He asked about Dick Poole, expecting he'd be dead, too, but Poole had been found, wounded, on the far shore, and two of the boys had risked their lives to go after him and save him for the hangman.

"Prison," he said. "Prison for anything Dick has done."

It was then he learned that Dick Poole had clubbed his uncle Clay to death. Clay had learned he was a spy, and had accused him, and Dick had ambushed him. Ax-Handle Ole had told it all, and he had told about Swiftwater, too.

Chipman went back to sleep. By morning he was himself again, up and around, looking at the drag end of the log drive with all but a few laggard sticks gone downriver.

He stood with Lynne beside him. He did not need her arm for support, but he did not object; it was good to have it there.

"Lynne!" he said, and she was in his arms.

Some of the boys were watching from the cookhouse. He did not care if they watched or not. He kissed her, and he held her in his arms for a long, long time.

THE END
of a novel by
Dan Cushman

Dan Cushman was born in Osceola, Michigan, and grew up on the Cree Indian reservation in Montana. He graduated from the University of Montana with a Bachelor of Science degree in 1934 and pursued a career in mining as a prospector, assayer, and geologist before turning to journalism. In the early 1940s his novelette-length stories began appearing regularly in such Fiction House magazines as *North-West Romances* and *Frontier Stories*. Later in the decade his North-Western and Western stories as well as fiction set in the Far East and Africa began appearing in *Action Stories*, *Adventure*, and *Short Stories*. A collection of some of his best North-Western and Western fiction has recently been published, *Voyageurs of the Midnight Sun* (1995), with a Foreword by John Jakes who cites Cushman as a major influence in his own work. The character Comanche John, a Montana road agent featured in numerous rollicking magazine adventures, also appears in Cushman's first novel, *Montana, Here I Be* (1950) and in two later novels. *Stay Away, Joe*, which first appeared in 1953, is an amusing novel about the mixture, and occasional collision, of Indian culture and Anglo-American culture among the Métis (French Indians) living on a reservation in Montana. The novel became a bestseller and remains a classic to this day, greatly loved especially by Indian peoples for its truthfulness and humor. Yet, while humor became Cushman's hallmark in such later novels as *The Old Copper Collar* (1957) and *Goodbye, Old Dry* (1959), he also produced significant historical fiction in *The Silver Mountain* (1957), concerned with the mining and politics of silver in Montana in the 1890s. This novel won a Gold Spur Award from the Western Writers of America. His fiction remains notable for its breadth, ranging all the way from a story of the cattle frontier in *Tall Wyoming* (1957) to a poignant and memorable portrait of small town life in Michigan just before the Great War in *The Grand and the Glorious* (1963). More recent fiction such as *Rusty Irons* (1984) combines both the humor for which he is best known and the darker hues to be found in *The Silver Mountain*. His most recent novels are *In Alaska With Shipwreck Kelly* (1995) and *Valley of the Thousand Smokes* (1996).